DREAMWORKS

TROLLHUNTERS
TALES OF ARCADIA
FROM GUILLERMO DEL TORO

AGE OF THE AMULET

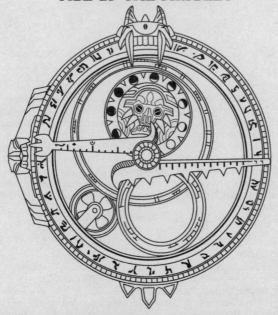

Written by Richard Ashley Hamilton
Based on characters from DreamWorks Tales of Arcadia series

Simon Spotlight
New York   London   Toronto   Sydney   New Delhi

SIMON SPOTLIGHT
An imprint of Simon & Schuster Children's Publishing Division
1230 Avenue of the Americas, New York, New York 10020
This Simon Spotlight paperback edition June 2018
DreamWorks Trollhunters © 2018 DreamWorks Animation LLC. All Rights Reserved. All rights reserved, including the right of reproduction in whole or in part in any form. SIMON SPOTLIGHT and colophon are registered trademarks of Simon & Schuster, Inc. For information about special discounts for bulk purchases, please contact Simon & Schuster Special Sales at 1-866-506-1949 or business@simonandschuster.com.
Designed by Jay Colvin
Manufactured in the United States of America 0518 OFF
10 9 8 7 6 5 4 3 2 1
ISBN 978-1-5344-1660-4 (hc)
ISBN 978-1-5344-1659-8 (pbk)
ISBN 978-1-5344-1661-1 (eBook)

SEEING RED

Tellad-Urr did not always hate being the Trollhunter.

There was a time, hundreds of years before, when receiving Merlin's Amulet seemed like receiving a gift. Despite the weight of the Daylight Armor, Tellad-Urr stood tall. His heart pumped with pride as he fought his sworn enemies, the Gumm-Gumms. His noble face smiled whenever the younger Trolls gathered around their hero. "Tellad-Urr the Triumphant!" they would cheer as he strode past. The Trollhunter loved that part the best.

Alas, that was centuries ago. That was before the Amulet's relentless ticking made Tellad-Urr's horns ache. Before the Daylight Armor bent his back with endless burden. Before his heart, once thundering with purpose, beat only out of habit. Before his face, now battle-worn and scarred, made a sneer of his smile. The younger Trolls barely noticed their triumphant hero anymore. Now they said nothing as he limped past. That part hurt the Trollhunter the most.

This morning was no different. Tellad-Urr desperately wanted to sleep. But the ticking Amulet would not let Tellad-Urr rest. Its blue light pulsed past his shut eyelids.

"Enough!" roared the Trollhunter.

Leaving the Amulet behind on purpose, he stormed into the underground city he was forced to protect: Trollmarket. Tellad-Urr passed the purple Heartstone, which hung from the cavern's ceiling like a jeweled stalactite, and hoped the other Trolls would ignore him, as usual.

"Ah, Trollhunter," said Kilfred, his fur striped black and white. "How good to see you."

Tellad-Urr stopped midstep, caught off guard, and asked, "Really? It . . . it *is*?"

"Of course," Kilfred answered warmly. "We just found another nest of Gnomes in SplitSkull's apothecary."

The brief hope in the Trollhunter's eyes dimmed.

"Filthy vermin," continued Kilfred, oblivious to Tellad-Urr's disappointment. "Almost as bad as humans. Though not nearly as tasty. I suggest bringing a shovel to scoop up their—"

Tellad-Urr gritted his teeth and stomped away from the striped Troll.

"Where are you going?" Kilfred called after him in confusion. "Was it something I said?"

Once the Horngazel tunnel closed behind him, Tellad-Urr let out a long, calming breath. He found himself on a grassy field on the surface world, surrounded by the ring of standing stone pillars he had erected during his rare downtime. Stonehenge, the humans had taken to calling it. The Trollhunter looked up at the sky. The sun had not yet risen, but it colored the horizon a deep shade of red. Red as flame. Red as blood.

In an existence filled with duty and discipline, this sight was the only thing that brought the Trollhunter a sense of relief—although he always had to leave right before the sunrise, lest his Troll body be turned to solid rock. Tellad-Urr sighed . . . before a familiar blue glow flashed in his eyes. The

Amulet shone in the grass before him. He seized the device and said, "I hate you."

"Finally," came a grim voice behind him. "Something we agree upon."

Tellad-Urr spun around. From the shadows of Stonehenge, a powerfully large Gumm-Gumm emerged, his fangs plainly visible in the overbite formed by his mismatched jaws.

"Orlagk the Oppressor," said Tellad-Urr. "Have you come to finally surrender your Gumm-Gumm army? Or are you here for another pointless battle?"

"My forces shall never surrender, Trollhunter," said Orlagk. "Even now, they train with my most brutal general, Gunmar. And as for battle, I assure you . . ."

The Gumm-Gumm flexed his claw, forcing strands of opaque energy to rise and weave into the jagged shape of a sword. Once it had solidified, Orlagk trained his Decimaar Blade on Tellad-Urr and said, "This one has a *point*."

The Trollhunter rolled his eyes and said, "For the glory of Merlin, *blah, blah, blah*."

The Amulet erupted. Brilliant streaks of light swirled around Tellad-Urr, lifting him. Metal plates appeared out of thin air and formed silver armor around his body. Tellad-Urr the Triumphant returned heavily to the ground, the Sword of Daylight materializing in his hand.

Orlagk sliced wildly with his Decimaar Blade. The Trollhunter braced himself and deflected the attacks, their swords sparking with each clash.

"Even you must realize you're on the wrong side of this war," growled Orlagk between slashes. "Forget Merlin and join me so that we might rule this world together, above and below!"

Tellad-Urr pushed away his enemy and said, "Mark my words, Orlagk. If I could forfeit this Amulet, I would. Not to aid you, but so that I might know a moment's peace."

"The only peace you'll find is in death!" yelled Orlagk with another stab.

The Trollhunter dodged, and the Amulet—now embedded in his breastplate—sent a wave of yellow light cascading along the armor's engravings. The surge ended at Tellad-Urr's free hand, creating a double-headed battle-ax.

"A new weapon," said Orlagk. "Loaded a new gemstone into your Amulet, have you?"

With a single slice of his ax, Tellad-Urr chopped down one of Stonehenge's pillars. A tall shadow fell over Orlagk as the stone slab toppled toward him. The Gumm-Gumm leaped out of the way just before the pillar flattened the ground behind him.

"Truth be told, I don't like humans any more than you do, Orlagk," said Tellad-Urr, readying the ax for another strike while Orlagk spit grass from his uneven mouth. "But the sooner I stop you from attacking them, the sooner this Amulet will leave me."

The Trollhunter stepped on Orlagk's hand—the one holding the Decimaar Blade—keeping him on the ground. The squirming Gumm-Gumm said, "And what then?"

Tellad-Urr's next words caught in his throat. He wasn't quite sure how to answer the question. The Trollhunter had spent so many years hoping the Amulet would go away, he never considered what he'd do if that wish was actually granted.

"Do you honestly think those cowering fleshbags will crawl out of their huts to thank you?" Orlagk continued. "Or that 'good' Trolls will suddenly sing of your triumphs again?"

The words injured Tellad-Urr worse than any weapon. The Trollhunter's sneer softened. His eyes welled with emotion, and he lowered his sword and ax as he reconsidered his existence. It was just the opportunity Orlagk sought.

In the span of a heartbeat, the Gumm-Gumm King made the Decimaar Blade vanish out of his pinned hand and reappear in his free one. Orlagk swung with all his might and sheared off the Trollhunter's left horn. Tellad-Urr crumpled in agony, the Sword of Daylight and the ax dissipating as he clutched his wound. It felt as if every nerve in his skull had been set ablaze.

"You don't seem so triumphant now." Orlagk smirked.

He kicked Tellad-Urr, sending him rolling out of Stonehenge and down the hill. After several bruising tumbles, the Trollhunter's body came to a rest in a gulch at the bottom. He could barely move. Orlagk loomed over him again, blotting out Tellad-Urr's view of the coming dawn.

"Either finish me, or leave me to my first—and last—sunrise," grunted the Trollhunter.

"I'll do neither, Trollhunter," Orlagk gloated.

"Just as I won't force you to my side."

The Gumm-Gumm held his sword less than an inch from Tellad-Urr's scarred face and said, "With but a scratch from my Decimaar Blade, I could make you my slave instead of that sorcerer's. But I'd rather see you suffer, Tellad-Urr. Well, suffer more than you already do. . . ."

Orlagk climbed to the top of the hill and considered his defeated enemy one last time. The first rays of sunlight threatened to filter through the pillars of Stonehenge behind him.

"The surface world will never know peace, Trollhunter," vowed Orlagk. "Nor shall you."

With that, Orlagk disappeared behind the hill, trailing a cold laugh as he went. Alone now, Tellad-Urr mustered what little strength he had left and pulled himself out of the gulch. He grimaced as each movement sent a new jolt of pain through him. The missing horn threw off his balance, but the Trollhunter eventually righted himself.

"Why, Merlin?" Tellad-Urr whispered to the rapidly brightening sky. "Why have you cursed me with this thankless mission?"

He tripped and came crashing down again to

his knees, making him shout, "WHY ME?"

The cry echoed across Stonehenge and beyond for quite some time. After it faded, a new voice said, "You know he won't answer."

Tellad-Urr discovered a new Gumm-Gumm in the shadow of the hill, studying him through two burning eyes. This one wasn't as big as Orlagk, yet he appeared far more dangerous.

"Gunmar," Tellad-Urr rasped. "I suppose you came to finish what your king started."

"Orlagk is a fool," said Gunmar, careful not to touch the shafts of sunlight creeping across the field. "He leads our armies to ruin. I, on the other hand, come bearing an offer. A *gift*."

Gunmar held out his claw and opened it, revealing a small red gem in his massive palm.

"Strange, is it not, how we each serve an unworthy master?" asked Gunmar. "But what if there was a way to *break* their hold over us? To reclaim control of our own fates once again?"

Tellad-Urr tried to look away, but his eyes remained riveted to the crimson gemstone. Gunmar saw this and bared his canines in an awful parody of a smile.

"Being the Trollhunter has brought you nothing but pain. Why not return the favor?" asked Gunmar, holding the red gem closer. "Why not be triumphant once more?"

Tellad-Urr watched his own hand reach out and take the gemstone from Gunmar. He unfastened the Amulet from his chest and said, "No. This isn't about triumph. . . ."

A small compartment opened on the back of the ticking device, as if in invitation. Tellad-Urr placed the gem inside and returned the Amulet to his breastplate.

The Trollhunter smiled for the first time in ages and said, "This is far more terrible."

A fiery wave of light now cascaded along the armor's engravings, causing the metal plates to shift and sharpen, turning them a deep shade of red. Red as the sunrise. Red as flame. Red as blood.

CHAPTER 1
KITCHEN CONFIDENTIAL

"Terrific," groaned Jim Lake Jr. in his kitchen. "This is just what I need after the week—the month—the *year* I've had!"

"I'm sorry," said Walter Strickler in mock chagrin. "Would you prefer we stop by later?"

Strickler and his companion, Ms. Nomura, shared a smirk and drank more tea. Jim yanked his mom's teacups out of their hands before they could take another sip and said, "I'd prefer it if I never see your double-faces again!"

"So, I'm guessing a refill's out of the question?" asked Nomura.

Jim rushed the cups over to the sink and began washing them. He really had to scrub at the stubborn smudge of Nomura's violet lipstick as he said,

"You sneaking into my house is out of the question! So please, for once in your incredibly long lives, do me a favor and get out."

"I daresay your hospitality has lessened somewhat of late, Young Atlas," Strickler said.

"Yeah, well, a visit to the Darklands will do that to you," said Jim, drying the teacups and nodding at Nomura. "Just ask my old 'cellmate' over there."

Strickler made a *May I?* motion before taking the teacups from Jim. As he returned them to the shelf, Strickler said, "After you spared my life and exiled me from Arcadia Oaks, I had quite a lot of time to reflect on the consequences of my actions. How . . . how is Barbara these days?"

"Fine, no thanks to you," Jim said, his voice rising. "I just got done convincing her I'm not the Trollhunter. And that you're just some creep who left town—not the Changeling who almost got her killed!"

"I see . . . ," Strickler muttered, his eyes still downcast.

"If she sees you here . . . if she remembers who I really am . . . it'll break her heart all over again. And I'm *not* gonna let that happen," Jim warned.

Nomura whistled and said, "You weren't kidding, Walter. This kid really does carry the weight of the world on his shoulders."

"Jim, I understand that I wronged you," Strickler resumed. "I was once your teacher and—I'd like to think—your friend. Clearly, I broke that trust, but I want to make it up to you. After all, who is more capable of change . . . than a Changeling?"

Walter Strickler instantly transformed from his human guise into his true form—that of a tall, reptilian Changeling. Reaching under his cloak, Strickler retrieved a green fistful of feather darts and flung them at Jim.

"Whoa!" Jim hollered, ducking the razor-sharp projectiles.

Tucking and rolling behind the kitchen island, Jim pulled the Amulet from his jeans and said in a single breath, "For-the-glory-of-Merlin-Daylight-is-mine-to-command!"

Strickler shielded his yellow eyes from the Amulet's glare. When the incandescence faded, Jim Lake Jr. stood before him, encased in the Daylight Armor of the Trollhunter. The shape-shifter lowered his arm and said, "Your reflexes remain as keen as ever. But how do you fare against two enemies at once?"

Jim turned around just in time to see Nomura's body morph into that of a lithe, purple Changeling. She snatched the meat cleaver and Santoku knife from the cutting board and hurled them at the Trollhunter. The Sword of Daylight manifested in Jim's hand, and he used the flat of his blade to deflect the two knives. The Santoku lodged into the ceiling, but Strickler caught the cleaver and closed in on Jim. Nomura pulled two scythes from the scabbards on her back.

Looks like close-quarters combat, thought Jim as he magically replaced the Sword of Daylight with his Glaives—a pair of curved throwing weapons, one in each of Jim's hands.

"This reminds me of the first time I was invited to dinner at your home," Strickler joked.

The two Glaives sparked against Nomura's and Strickler's blades as Jim parried their every strike like a skilled swashbuckler. Sandwiched between two bloodthirsty shape-shifters, Jim's mind raced. He knew his coordination would falter eventually and that Strickler and Nomura would carve him up like a Thanksgiving turkey. So rather than keep the Changelings *away* from him, the Trollhunter hooked his Glaives around their weapons and pulled them *toward* him. Strickler and Nomura slammed into each other and fell to the tiled floor in a heap. Kicking away the scythes and cleaver, Jim said, "Nobody beats me in the kitchen. *Nobody.*"

"Cheers, Young Atlas," Strickler said. "You passed this pop quiz with flying colors."

"Pop quiz?!" Jim bellowed. "You two just tried to filet me with my own knives!"

"Just imagine what Gunmar will do now that he's out of the Darklands," said Nomura.

"Do you think he'll hesitate to send every Gumm-Gumm at his disposal after you? Just because of the week—the month—the *year* you've had?" Strickler added sharply.

"You . . . you . . . ," Jim stammered in outrage, until he closed his eyes and took a steadying breath. "You're right."

Strickler and Nomura looked at each other, cocking their eyebrows in surprise.

"Why would I ever expect my enemies to come after me one at a time? I've never been that lucky,"

Jim added, then looked at the Amulet on his chest. "Not since this thing found me."

He picked up the discarded meat cleaver and muttered, "All I wanted to do tonight was relax at home, cook a nice dinner for my mom, and maybe even get my homework done for a change. For once—just once—I wish this Amulet would let me do what *I* wanted."

"And so it can, Young Atlas," said Strickler, reverting to his human visage. "I can show you how . . . *if* you accept me as your teacher again."

A genuine smile spread across Strickler's face, prompting Jim to actually consider the offer . . . until a set of headlights danced across the kitchen walls. Hearing a car pull into the driveway, Jim cried, "Oh no—my mom's home!"

"Barbara?" Strickler whispered to himself.

"Go! Through the back door!" Jim ordered.

Nomura collected her scythes and stopped in front of Jim to say, "You have a lovely home. Sorry I didn't mention it the last time I was here, trying to kill you."

With that, Nomura adopted her human disguise and slinked into the twilit backyard. Strickler reluctantly followed, but hesitated at the threshold to address Jim one last time.

"I know I have hurt you. Your friends. Your family," Strickler said in quiet apology. "But at least consider what I said, Jim."

Before Jim could respond, Walter Strickler slipped outside. No sooner did the back door close than the front one opened. Barbara Lake stepped into the entryway and called, "Jim, I'm home. My shift ended early. Isn't that great?"

In the kitchen, Jim wiped the sweat from his forehead with the back of his arm, only to be reminded that he was still holding the meat cleaver. And still wearing his armor.

"Uh, yeah!" Jim lied, his voice going up an octave. "Great!"

As Jim raced toward the knife block, Barbara threw her white doctor's coat on the sofa. She crossed over to the dining room, missing the tail end of a mystical light show before she reached the kitchen and found her son. Jim stood ramrod straight in his normal clothes, a strained smile on his face and the Amulet tucked into his back pocket.

"How was your day?" Barbara asked.

"Uneventful?" said Jim, still sweating profusely.

"Uneventful is good," Barbara said. "But what was that blue light I just saw?"

"Um, maybe a glare?" Jim suggested lamely. "From your . . . lenses?"

Barbara shrugged, removed her eyeglasses, and cleaned them with the fabric of her hospital scrubs. Jim looked to the heavens and allowed himself a small sigh of relief. That's when he noticed the Santoku still wedged in the ceiling, directly over his mom's head. With mounting dread, Jim saw the knife start to slip lower and lower, until it finally came loose and fell—right toward Barbara. She had barely put on her glasses before Jim yanked her forward.

"Wha—Jim?!" Barbara yelped.

Jim pulled his mom into a hug with one arm and, with his free hand, he caught the knife by its handle behind them. Barbara's surprise gave way to happiness. She hugged her son in return and said, "And here I was worrying that you were getting too old for these."

"Never, Mom," Jim replied from the bottom of his heart.

Barbara squeezed her son a little tighter before

she let him go. Jim subtly returned the Santoku to the knife block without his mom seeing and said, "Now, what would you say to a nice, home-cooked meal of grilled polenta cakes served under a hearty mushroom ragout and accompanied by a side of sautéed kale with crispy garlic and chilies?"

"I would say that sounds delish—" Barbara began before a buzz interrupted her.

"This is Gun Robot. You have a text message," announced Jim's ringtone.

"Ah, it's just Tobes," said Jim, pulling out his cell phone. "He probably wants . . ." He trailed off as he read the text:

JIMBO! COME QUICK!! YOU KNOW WHERE!!!

". . . to ruin my evening," Jim finished under his breath.

"What's that, honey?" Barbara asked, not quite hearing that last part.

Recovering, Jim said, "Toby's, um, just reminded me that I promised to help with our *Español* homework tonight. But I can probably just blow him off . . ."

Jim's cell phone buzzed with another text from Toby:

DUDE! IT'S CRAZY-TOWN BANANA-PANTS! I REPEAT:

CRAZY-TOWN BANANA-PANTS!!!!!!!!!!!!!!!!!!!!!!!!!!!!!!!!!!!!!!

"Or not," Jim added, scrolling through the thousands of exclamation points Toby typed.

"Go help your friend," Barbara said. "Besides, I'm sure the last thing a teenager wants to do is spend the night at home with his mother."

"Actually . . . ," Jim started, still scrolling through exclamation points.

But before Jim could finish the thought, Barbara kissed him on the cheek and rummaged through the refrigerator for leftovers. Jim's cell buzzed with yet another Toby text:

S.U.C.

Jim immediately recognized that acronym. It was a secret code he and Toby used only in case of extreme emergencies. They came up with it after the time Jim wore a Grit-Shaka—a Troll relic that turned him into a carefree, albeit unbearably overconfident, jerk.

Seriously un-crispy.

"Why me?" Jim Lake Jr. asked of no one in particular.

CHAPTER 2
HERDING CATS

"Oh my gosh oh my gosh oh my gosh oh my gosh!" fretted Toby Domzalski as he shifted his weight from foot to foot in front of an abandoned warehouse.

Moonlight reflected off its broken windows, and overgrown weeds stood almost as tall as Toby's squat, antsy body. He nervously unwrapped a Nougat Nummie and stuffed it into his mouth just as Jim motored around the corner on his Vespa. Squeezing on the brakes, Jim brought his scooter to a halt in front of his best friend and stowed his helmet under the seat.

"Im! Uhtookoo tho wong?" garbled Toby through nougat-gummed braces.

"I got here as fast as I could!" Jim said, having learned long ago how to understand Toby when his mouth was full of candy, which was frequently.

"Is this what you texted me about?" Jim asked Toby, scanning between the trees for danger. "Is the warehouse under attack already?"

"Nope," Toby said from behind Jim. "At least, not from the *outside*. It's . . . well, you gotta come in quick so you can see for yourself. You won't believe your—"

"Duck!" Jim shouted, pushing Toby aside.

Jim's Amulet highlighted two small spheres that landed beside them and started spewing thick plumes of smoke. Using the smokescreen as cover, Steve Palchuk leaped out of the woods and said, "The jig's up, losers! You've just been caught—"

"By the Creepslayerz!" Eli Pepperjack finished as he jumped right next to Steve.

Toby traded a confused look with Jim, then said, "Y'know, that would've been *a lot* cooler if your smoke bombs actually worked."

Steve and Eli looked down, seeing how the smoke never rose above Jim and Toby's feet.

"You mean, it didn't seem like we appeared out of thin air?" Eli asked, adjusting his glasses.

Steve kicked away the sputtering smoke bombs

like they were two tiny soccer balls and yelled, "I told you these were lame!"

"Maybe we can return them to the magic shop," said Eli. "My mom saved the receipt!"

Jim pointed at the unlikely duo and asked, "Are you two . . . hanging out now?"

"None of your business, Lake!" Steve said. "But do you know what *our* business is?"

"Making unnecessarily dramatic entrances?" guessed Toby.

"No, *Dumb*zalski!" Steve snapped. "Our business is finding out what you and those . . . those Trolls have been up to all this time!"

"You did promise to answer a few thousand questions, Jim," Eli reminded him.

"You're right," Jim said. "I owe you that. Okay, it all started when I got this Amulet—"

He paused when the warehouse's last intact window shattered above them. A little green Changeling flew out of the building and landed on his diapered rear next to Steve and Eli.

"What're you two glorks lookin' at?" barked NotEnrique as he dusted himself off.

"Maybe I should explain on the go," Jim

suggested as Toby opened the warehouse door.

The stunned Creepslayerz followed Jim, Toby, and NotEnrique inside, only for their jaws to drop in surprise. Thousands upon thousands of Trolls filled the building, hefting large wooden crates and shouting at one another in Trollspeak. Some Trolls yanked cinderblocks out of the walls to build make-shift caves. Some chased hungrily after the stray cats that lived in the warehouse. And some merely hung from the rafters, chugging foamy, sloshing mugs of glug.

"I see what you mean, Tobes," said Jim, side-stepping a glug spill. *"Seriously un-crispy."*

"The Trolls've been like this ever since we brought them to the surface," Toby explained.

"Start talking before I start punching, Lake," Steve said.

"Fair enough," Jim replied, now wading through the chaos around them. "I think you know the basics by now, but long story short: Trolls have lived in secret beneath us for thousands of years. They're usually friendly—"

"So long as you fleshbags keep yer distance," NotEnrique said.

"Although there are exceptions. Not to mention the seriously evil Trolls we're on the run from—the Gumm-Gumms," said Jim, his brow knitted in worry. "They're led by this maniac, Gunmar, who wants nothing less than to destroy every human and rule the world."

"Oh, and to make an ocean of blood from Jim's loved ones," Toby chimed in helpfully.

"Right, how could I forget?" Jim said with an eye roll. "Anyway, Gunmar used to be trapped in another dimension called the Darklands . . . until a few days ago. But now that he's taken over the Trolls' home, we've had to relocate them up here. Which we couldn't have done without the . . . uh, *Creepslayerz*? That's *really* what you're calling yourselves?"

"So all this time, when you've been sneaking off with Domzalski and Nuñez . . ."

"We've been trying to stop Gunmar," Toby said, dodging a Troll that was chasing a cat. "Just like all the other Trollhunters who came before Jim. Only, lately, we haven't been doing so hot."

"Great Gronka Morka!" said a familiar voice, making Jim and Toby turn around.

Blinky stepped out of the mass of stir-crazy Trolls, followed by his gigantic companion, AAARRRGGHH!!!

"Hey, Blink. Hey, Wingman," greeted Toby, fist-bumping all four of Blinky's hands, then AAARRRGGHH!!!'s two massive paws.

Eli tentatively touched the runes etched along AAARRRGGHH!!!'s powerful arms, and whispered, "Whoa . . . stone for skin. And it's warm!"

"Tickles," giggled AAARRRGGHH!!!

"So, how's your first day on the job, oh fearless Troll leader?" Toby asked Blinky.

"Heavy is the head that wears the crown, Tobias," answered the six-eyed Troll. "We've been sorting through all the crates of Troll artifacts RotGut could carry. But getting a warehouse full of Trolls to follow orders is like . . . what's the human expression? Ah yes—herding cats!"

"Cats?" asked a passing Troll, licking his lips in anticipation. "Where?"

"Not now, Plagsnork!" griped Blinky before going back to massaging his temples. "It pains me to admit it, but I'll never be the leader Vendel was. Or Rundle, and Kilfred before him."

"Ah, you'll do great, Blink," Jim said. "After all, you've been a great teacher to me."

Speaking of teachers, Jim had wanted to tell Blinky about his recent run-in with Strickler. But now Jim figured the news could wait, seeing his six-eyed friend so harried by his new duties. After all, the Trollhunter knew all too well what it felt like to be overwhelmed by responsibility.

"Penny for your thoughts, Romeo," came a new, somewhat tired, voice.

Jim roused back to the present and saw Claire Nuñez leaning against her Shadow Staff like a crutch. She smiled, her eyes sparkling despite the dark, puffy bags under them.

He hugged her and said, "So, what'd your parents think of your new hairdo?"

Jim ran his fingers through a bone-white lock of Claire's otherwise black hair. The streak had always been dyed blue . . . until she transported half of Trollmarket's population to Arcadia with her Shadow Staff. The strain of such a feat had somehow bleached her hair from blue to white, although Jim thought Claire looked great in any color.

"Haven't shown them yet." Claire yawned. "I've

just been hanging out here at Troll-a-palooza until I get my strength back from that shadow-jump."

"But that was hours ago," Jim said. "Maybe my mom should give you a checkup—"

A booming crash interrupted Jim. Two distracted Trolls had collided and dropped the heavy crates they were carrying. The wooden boxes smashed to the ground, scattering Troll goods across the warehouse floor—as well as a nest of stowaway Gnomes. The sight of their pointy red hats whipped the Trolls into a brand-new frenzy, causing them overturn more crates and demolish more of the warehouse. When a couple of the Gnomes skittered under Steve's shirt, he shrieked, "Ew! Ew! Ew! Get 'em off, Eli!"

Eli tried to catch the squirrely critters—only to grab their hats, exposing huge horns underneath. NotEnrique roared with more laughter, while Jim and Team Trollhunters attempted to corral the Gnomes and quell the panic spreading across the warehouse.

I just wanted dinner with Mom, thought Jim as he pried an addled Gnome from his scalp and looked out at the pandemonium raging around him.

In the confusion, the Creepslayerz backed into

a teetering stack of RotGut's crates and accidentally toppled them. An oddly shaped Troll contraption tumbled out of one of the boxes and smashed against the concrete floor.

"A Kairosect!" Jim said, recognizing the damaged device. "Guys, we can use this to pause time and put these pointy little Gnome genies back in their bottle!".

"A splendid strategy, Master Jim!" hollered Blinky, holding four wriggling Gnomes in each of his hands. "Although its effects last only forty-three minutes and nine seconds—and I seriously question whether that's long enough to put an end to this magnitude of madness!"

The Trollhunter bent over to retrieve the Kairosect. But before he could touch it, an arc of green electricity jumped out of its cracked casing. Jim recoiled his hand as more and more strange energy currents sparked from the Kairosect's exposed inner workings.

"Um, I don't think it's supposed to do that," Toby said.

Jim pushed Steve and Eli clear of the expanding energy's radius and said, "We need to contain this,

this—whatever it is—before it spreads to the rest of the warehouse!"

"One shadow portal, coming up!" Claire replied as she raised her staff and generated a black hole above the malfunctioning mechanism.

But the Kairosect's seeping energies mingled unpredictably with the Shadow Staff's magic, causing the portal to enlarge and spread around Team Trollhunters. The Trolls in the warehouse took cover behind more clusters of crates, but Jim stood fast. Over the roar of the wind rushing into the vacuum, he shouted, "Claire! Can you shut it down?"

"I'm trying!" Claire said through gritted teeth. "But the Shadow Staff isn't responding!"

"I've said it before and I'll say it again—Great Gronka Morka!" cried Blinky as the cyclonic portal swept him into the air.

"Wingman!" AAARRRGGHH!!! called after Toby as they, too, disappeared into the dark tornado, followed by Claire.

I guess dinner with Mom's gonna have to wait a bit longer, thought Jim before he leaped headfirst into the same black vortex that consumed his friends.

CHAPTER 3
CLONK-DONK

Jim felt his body land on supple grass instead of the hard cement he was expecting. Opening one eye and then the other, he saw that the warehouse and the disgruntled Trolls within it had disappeared— only to be replaced by unspoiled green hills as far as the eye could see.

"I have a feeling I'm not in Arcadia anymore," Jim said, his breath visible in the night air.

"Or North America, for that matter," replied Blinky from a nearby treetop, pulling twigs from his hair. "By my estimation, we've arrived, most uncomfortably, in the moors of England."

"England?" Jim marveled. "Blink, how can you be sure?"

"Blinky from here," AAARRRGGHH!!! said as

he appeared over the next hill, carrying Toby and Claire on his back. "Well, under it."

The gentle giant lowered Toby and Claire, and they both rushed over to Jim. Everyone seemed to be unhurt for the most part, although Claire looked somewhat pale.

"Correct," said Blinky as he climbed down the tree. "I grew up around these parts ages ago, in the *original* Trollmarket beneath the fabled hill of Arthurian legend, Glastonbury Tor."

"But I've never been to England," Claire said with a queasy shudder. "I have no emotional connection to this place. So how'd my Shadow Staff teleport us here?"

"Hmm, a valid query," Blinky conceded.

"Well, let's answer it *after* we've gotten back home," Claire said, extending her Shadow Staff once more. "Right now, I could go for a hot bath and a couple of aspirin."

Focusing her mind on the staff, she mentally commanded it to open a new portal . . . but nothing happened. Claire tried again, but still nothing.

"Maybe you're just tired," said Jim, putting a consoling arm around her. "You're clearly fighting off some kind of bug and reeling from two massive shadow-jumps in a row."

"Then perhaps our best course of action is to reconnoiter," Blinky said.

"Raccoon-oyster?" AAARRRGGHH!!! said.

"Reconnoiter," Blinky corrected. "A human word that means: to search, scout, or survey one's surroundings."

"Ah," AAARRRGGHH!!! grumbled in understanding. "A look-see."

Toby pulled out his cell phone and said, *"No problemo.* Allow me to simply open my handy-dandy ride-sharing app and hail us a . . ."

Toby's cheerful voice trailed off as he noticed that his cell had no signal. Claire and Jim checked their phones and similarly found no signal bars. Their clocks and GPS-enabled maps weren't functioning either. Jim scratched his head and said, "We get reception deep inside of Gatto's gut, but *not* out here in the open?"

The quintet trudged along the moors. To Jim, walking in the fields of heather felt like walking in a dream. Maybe it was because Claire and his best friends were beside him. Maybe it was because he'd never been this far from home before. Or maybe it was because of all the . . .

"Smoke," AAARRRGGHH!!! said, sniffing the air.

Team Trollhunters crested the next hill, only to stop short in their tracks. Below them sat a small, ramshackle village comprised of a few mud huts surrounded by a wooden guard wall. They saw no cars, for there were no roads, nor did there appear to be any power lines. The only signs of life came from the few people in rags who pushed wheelbarrows along the village's rutted pathways.

"Yeesh," Toby said. "It looks like the past few centuries completely skipped over this place!"

"In point of fact, Tobias, I fear it is *we* who have skipped a few centuries!" said Blinky.

They all traded surprised looks before Jim said, "Blinky, are you telling us that Claire's portal not only sent us halfway around the world—but also clonk-donked us into the *past*?"

"Indeed, Master Jim, that is the only scenario that makes sense to me at this moment," Blinky uttered gravely. "Except for the 'clonk-donk' part. I have no idea what that means."

"It's this weird sound effect they make on that TV show we told you about, *Mistrial & Error*," Claire explained. "Every time the scene changes, the audience hears a—"

"Clonk-donk," AAARRRGGHH!!! filled in.

"Sorry I asked," Blinky muttered. "But yes, for all intents and purposes, it would appear that the Shadow Staff's arcane magic somehow reacted— quite adversely—with the ruptured Kairosect to, er, *clonk-donk* us backward through time! Metaphysically speaking, of course."

Jim looked back at the village and found the source of the smoke: a fire pit upon which a cauldron of stew bubbled. The tantalizing smell made him think of dinner which, in turn, made Jim think of his mom alone at home, probably eating a microwave burrito for dinner. Pushing the sad image from his mind, he said, "I know we're all probably wondering how we're gonna get back. But first things first, we need to find food, warmth, and shelter for Blink and AAARRRGGHH!!! before the sun comes up."

"A most prudent course of action," agreed Blinky as he, AAARRRGGHH!!!, Toby, and Claire followed Jim down the hill and toward the village.

They soon reached the outer wall, which had been constructed from thick logs and lit with torches at regular intervals around the perimeter. In the flickering light, Jim saw two sheets billowing on a nearby clothesline. He pulled them down, handed them to his two Troll friends, and said, "Hopefully, the locals won't mind us borrowing their laundry."

Blinky and AAARRRGGHH!!! donned the sheets, wearing them like cloaks to conceal their bodies. AAARRRGGHH!!! tucked his horns under the fabric and asked, "How we look?"

"Better than me. I don't think braces are gonna be invented for another millennium!" said Toby, the metal in his mouth glinting in the torches' glow.

Jim approached the village's front gate, expecting it to be barricaded, but found it open. Oddly, whatever metal hardware used to bar the entrance had been stripped away—violently so, judging by the splintered wood on the hinges. Team Trollhunters slipped past the unlocked gate and stole over to the hamlet's fire pit, warming their chilled bodies. Jim closed his eyes, feeling the comforting heat along his face before he felt four sharp points dig into his back.

Startled, Jim and his friends spun around and found themselves surrounded by a dozen grime-streaked villagers, all holding farm tools like weapons. One of them poked with his wooden pitchfork again and demanded something in a dialect Jim didn't quite understand.

"What language are they speaking?" Blinky asked, his four hands raised in surrender.

"It's Old English," Claire decided after hearing a few more of their words.

"Like Shakespeare?" said Toby. "Something tells me these guys aren't theater buffs!"

"Shakespeare wrote in Modern English!" Claire pointed out.

"That's my Juliet," Jim quipped.

"Indeed!" said Blinky. "And Claire's keen linguistic talents have also pinpointed our setting to sometime in the Dark Ages."

"Sounds unpleasant," AAARRRGGHH!!! said as a villager's club broke against his back.

"Maybe my Amulet can help translate what they're saying," said Jim.

He flipped over the device in his hand and watched its outer ring spin. As it whirled, the

37

incantation engraved into the dial shifted from Modern English letters to Latin to . . . gibberish.

"That's never happened before," said Jim, staring at jumbled mess of characters. "Let's try this again. For the glory of Merlin, Daylight is mine to command!"

Numerous orbs of mystical energy erupted from the Amulet's core. The phosphorescent balls criss-crossed around Jim, erecting the Daylight Armor around his body and the Sword of Daylight into his hand. Jim swung the blade in wide arcs, making the frightened villagers back off.

"Your welcoming committee needs a little work," Jim told them. "I don't know if you can understand me, but my friends and I come in peace. We're Trollhunters—"

Every single villager wailed in horror at the sound of that last word. But before he could ask why, the Amulet flickered. Jim watched in alarm as his Daylight Armor abruptly fizzled into nothingness and the Amulet, now inert, plopped into the mud at his feet.

"What's going on with this thing?" Jim complained as he retrieved the device.

"And did you see our pitchforky pals' faces

when Jim said 'Trollhunter'?" Toby added.

"Not happy," said AAARRRGGHH!!!

"Oh no," whispered Blinky, his six eyes wide with fear. "By Gorgus, it can't be . . ."

"'Oh no' *what*, Blink?" asked Jim.

"I pray I'm mistaken," said Blinky. "That we haven't just landed in the worst possible place at the worst possible time. My friends, don't think me a coward, but we must run before . . ."

"Before what?" Claire asked, then got her answer.

The village's outer wall exploded inward with a deafening *BOOM*. Splintered logs rained down around Team Trollhunters, and the villagers scattered in horror. Once the dust settled, Jim, Claire, Toby, Blinky, and AAARRRGGHH!!! saw a red figure cross through the demolished defenses. A lone horn crowned his head, and armor hung in jagged crimson plates over his imposing form. Blinky found his voice and gasped, "It's him—it's Tellad-Urr the Terrible!"

CHAPTER 4
CREEPED OUT

"What's got everyone's diapers in a twist?" hiccuped NotEnrique.

The little Changeling had only now emerged from the bathtub full of glug in which he'd spent the last few minutes. Across the warehouse, the Creepslayerz finally stopped screaming as the shadow portal closed. They stumbled to the empty spot where Team Trollhunters once stood, finding only the Kairosect's battered remnants.

"I always thought Lake was a dweeb, but I never wanted him to, y'know, get sucked into a black hole of death," said Steve.

"We shall avenge you, Jim!" shouted Eli, thrusting his fists into the air. "So swears Elijah Leslie Pepperjack!"

"*That's* yer name?" NotEnrique snorted, trailing tiny footprint puddles as he approached. "Who filled out the birth certificate—yer worst enemy?"

The green imp then shook his entire body like a wet dog might, spraying Steve and Eli with glug droplets. But before they could complain, several large Trolls gathered around them.

"What're we supposed to do now?" said Bagdwella. "First, we're forced out of Heartstone Trollmarket, and now our Trollhunters have disappeared!"

"At least these two are okay," Rot said, pointing to Steve and Eli.

"Are you dense, Rot?" Gut scowled beside him. "This's all *their* fault!"

An angry murmur spread across the Trolls, many of them casting menacing glances at Steve and Eli. The Creepslayerz backed away, whispering out of the corners of their mouths.

"I'll sacrifice myself so you can get away, Steve," Eli said. "Tell our story to the world!"

Steve looked at Eli, seeing at him in a whole new light. He wanted to say so many things, but ultimately settled on, "Okay."

"That . . . that's it?" Eli asked, dejected. "Not even a 'thank you, Eli'?"

Steve's uncaring façade finally cracked, and he blurted out, "Ugh, fine! 'Creepslayerz never leave a man behind.' Is that what you wanted to hear, Eli?"

"*There's* the Steve I know!" cheered Eli.

"And this isn't our fault!" Steve then shouted to the oncoming Trolls. "You creeps wanna blame something for your missing, unmuscular hero? Blame this!"

Steve kicked the lifeless Kairosect with his sneaker. The oncoming Trolls halted at once, and a confident grin spread across Steve's face—until the Kairosect sparked to life again.

"Steve, I don't mean to be a nagging nelly, but this time *is* your fault," whimpered Eli.

NotEnrique, the Trolls, and the Creepslayerz all stared in awe as the Kairosect spat out a new swirling shadow portal. It crackled with more of that peculiar green electricity, and the silhouettes of five figures—three small, two large—stepped out of the storming abyss.

"It's them!" whooped Eli. "They're back!"

The portal then reduced into a tiny black pinprick,

and the Kairosect detonated into hundreds of tiny fragments. Once the shrapnel stopped flying, the Trolls rushed up to their returned heroes—only to find that the five figures weren't Team Trollhunters at all. One of the new arrivals, a Troll coated with black-and-white fur, said, "What manner of trickery be this?"

"Kilfred?" said Bagdwella, recognizing the striped Troll.

With an awed hush, everyone bowed before Kilfred and his four companion Trolls—everyone, that is, except for Steve, Eli, and NotEnrique. The elfin Changeling pointed at Kilfred and said, "Who invited the talking zebra?"

"Bite your tongue, *Impure*!" bellowed Bagdwella. "This is Kilfred, father of Rundle, father of Vendel. One of the wisest advisors Trollkind has ever known. . . ."

"Where are my son and young grandson?" asked Kilfred, still disoriented. "Surely they can divine the reason for our sudden appearance here. One moment, my four students and I are tending to the Heartstone at Glastonbury Tor. The next, we find ourselves in this strange place."

"I dunno how to break this to ya," began NotEnrique. "But Vendel just got eighty-sixed by that backstabbin' Krubera, Queen Usurna!"

"What heresy is this?" wailed Kilfred. "My own kin . . . felled by enemy hands?"

"And Rundle sadly passed before Deya delivered us to the New World," said Bagdwella.

As she and the other Trolls welcomed the shell-shocked Kilfred and his four compatriots, Eli said, "Steve, do you realize what this means?! It means that Jim and the others might still be alive! This Kilfred character clearly lived a while ago, yet he and his students arrived here in the same kind of portal thingy that took our friends. If *he's* in the present, then maybe *they're* stuck in the past! It's just like that episode of *Sally Go-Back* where she had to switch places with Gun Robot to restore balance to the space-time continuum!"

"These are grave tidings, indeed," Kilfred said to the Trolls that gathered around him in rapt attention. "As I understand everything you've told me, Trolls have been evicted from their rightful place beneath the earth and left without a leader for the first instance in their long history."

"Then Gorgus has sent you here in our hour of greatest need, oh wise Kilfred. You must advise us once more," said Bagdwella, offering him the staff Blinky inherited from Vendel.

Kilfred looked at the wooden stick, which had been decorated with Christmas lights, and said, "What's this piece of junk? Where's the ceremonial Heartstone Staff that's been in my family for generations?"

"We, uh, we traded it for a recipe," NotEnrique admitted.

"So be it," announced Kilfred, accepting the junk staff. "I shall lead you, and, together, we shall restore Trollkind to its former glory!"

The assembled Trolls roared so loudly in approval, Steve and Eli jumped. The sudden movement reminded Kilfred of their presence. He pointed his new staff at the two humans and said, "Now let's start by eating those two!"

The Creepslayerz turned to each other and started screaming again.

CHAPTER 5
A TALE OF TWO AMULETS

Villagers screamed and ran past the stunned Jim, Toby, Claire, Blinky, and AAARRRGGHH!!! as Tellad-Urr the Terrible strode into their hamlet. Jim took a step toward this era's Trollhunter, only to be held back by four matching hands.

"Blinky, what're you doing?" Jim asked. "That's the Trollhunter. Well, a Trollhunter. If he's Merlin's creation in this time, then maybe he can help us get back to our own!"

"Bring me my tribute, fleshbags!" roared Tellad-Urr. "Or I shall burn down every single one of your pathetic huts and torture any foolish enough to look upon my blighted visage!"

"I don't know why they call this guy 'terrible,'" said Toby as the trembling villagers began wheeling their barrows toward the scarlet figure. "He seems pretty effective to me!"

"Tellad-Urr was not terrible in skill, Tobias," Blinky explained. "He was—is—so named for his ability to strike terror in the hearts of his victims. This is all stated in *A Brief Recapitulation of Troll Lore*, had you bothered to study it!"

"'Merlin's *mis*creation,'" Claire remembered from her reading. "Tellad-Urr was the only Trollhunter to ever use the Amulet for evil! Until he was defeated by Gogun the . . . something?"

"Gogun the Gentle," Blinky confirmed. "Tellad-Urr's successor and one of the bravest Trollhunters to ever wield the Amulet. Even Kanjigar looked up to Gogun's noble example."

Jim looked back at Tellad-Urr, his heart torn between revulsion and a creeping curiosity.

"Master Jim, you have only known the Trollhunters as allies," Blinky continued. "But Tellad-Urr is an enemy unlike any you have ever encountered. What horrible coincidence to have arrived at this exact time and place before Gogun has stopped him and restored order."

Jim looked down at the dormant Amulet in his

hand and said, "I know I haven't been a Trollhunter for long. But, so far, I haven't come across too much coincidence . . . only destiny."

He and his friends then watched the last villager leave the last wheelbarrow at Tellad-Urr's crimson booted feet. The dark Trollhunter looked down upon his tribute and grimaced.

"Is this is all?" he sneered in disappointment. "Is this how little you think of me?"

Tellad-Urr beckoned the Sundown Mace into his hand, its spiked ball as red as the rest of his abominable armor. The weapon then burst into flames, and he touched its lit end to a nearby thatched roof. Jim's eyes rounded in sorrow as it, and the village hut beneath it, started to burn.

"Good Gizmodius!" Blinky exclaimed. "He's loaded Magmar the Molten's Conflagration Stone into his own infernal Amulet!"

"His Amulet," said Jim, getting an idea. "It's like the heart of any Trollhunter. Maybe Tellad-Urr *doesn't* want to be this way. Maybe his Amulet . . . I don't know, called out to mine for help. Sorta like one of Claire's emotional anchors. Maybe *we're* supposed to stop this."

"But what about that Gogun guy?" asked Toby. "Isn't he the one who's supposed to take down Tellad-Urr?"

"Tobias raises a point of the utmost importance," said Blinky. "While I applaud your conviction, Master Jim, we simply cannot tamper with past events. Why, even our mere presence here could serve to undo history as we know it!"

"History is written by the victors," Jim heard himself say while moving toward the fire.

He marched through the smoke and embers, recalling how Strickler used to recite that Winston Churchill quote all the time in AP World History. Jim thought, *Man, that seems like a lifetime ago. Back when I only had to worry about normal teenage responsibilities.*

"Who's Victor?" asked AAARRRGGHH!!!

"I'll tell you later," Blinky sighed in resignation. "Provided that we don't destroy the very fabric of reality with a time paradox!"

The two Trolls removed their cloaks and joined Toby and Claire in following Jim's path toward Tellad-Urr the Terrible. The dark Trollhunter looked upon the five approaching strangers with impassive eyes.

"Tobes, please tell me you packed your Warhammer," said Jim.

Toby reached behind his back and pulled a hefty crystal mallet from his waistband. As the handle telescoped to its full length, he replied, "Never leave home without it."

"And I think I'm getting my second wind," said Claire, extending her Shadow Staff. "How about we put out those flames with an 'alley-oop,' AAARRRGGHH!!!?"

"On it," said AAARRRGGHH!!!

The large Troll picked up a pair of water troughs by the stable and hurled them into the air. Claire concentrated and formed two much smaller shadow-portals. The troughs flew through the first black hole and came out of the second—dousing the burning hut in one fell swoop.

Jim wanted to say, "Good going, guys!" But Tellad-Urr's hand whipped around to grasp his windpipe with such speed, Jim couldn't utter the first syllable. Gasping for air, he looked down and saw his denim-covered legs dangling a couple of feet off the village's pockmarked turf.

Claire, Toby, Blinky, and AAARRRGGHH!!! ran to

Jim's aid, but stopped short as Tellad-Urr applied more pressure to his throat. They seethed in place, calculating the next move.

"Where did you find that trinket?" said the dark Trollhunter, his eyes on Jim's Amulet.

"It found *me*," choked Jim.

"You're no Trollhunter," snarled Tellad-Urr. "For there will be no more Trollhunters after me. I'll not allow Merlin's curse to afflict another—"

Jim's Amulet suddenly went haywire, its gears no longer stalled but now whirring faster than they ever had before. Both Trollhunters, old and new, watched in confusion as lambent energy drifted out of Tellad-Urr's Amulet—and poured into Jim's.

"*That's* why Master Jim's Amulet malfunctioned," marveled Blinky, spellbound by the exchange. "Two Amulets cannot operate simultaneously. Merlin's magic won't be shared!"

The others remained entranced by the flow of siphoned energy, but Tellad-Urr had seen enough. He released Jim, breaking the link between the Amulets, and shouted, "Enough!"

AAARRRGGHH!!!, Blinky, Toby, and Claire helped Jim up. His partially recharged Amulet blinked and ticked sporadically. Tellad-Urr stalked around them in a circle, never taking his eyes off the foreign boy who somehow stole a fraction of his own strength.

"Tellad-Urr the Terrible, formerly Tellad-Urr the Triumphant!" Blinky addressed the dark Trollhunter. "We outnumber you five-to-one!"

"Is that so?" Tellad-Urr said before tapping the hijacked device on his chest.

The Amulet flushed with pink light in response, and four more Tellad-Urrs sprang into spontaneous existence beside the original. The identical savages rushed Team Trollhunters.

"Looks like he's got the Aspectus Stone, too," wheezed Jim. "I hate that thing."

Two of the Tellad-Urr duplicates tackled Blinky and AAARRRGGHH!!!, while two more snared Toby and Claire. This left Jim to face off alone against the first Tellad-Urr. Without his armor, Jim felt practically naked under the dark Trollhunter's withering glare.

"You may claim to be from tomorrow," said Tellad-Urr. "But you die today."

Tellad-Urr the Terrible swung his Sundown Mace. Jim's twitching Amulet went bonkers and spewed out what little energy it had taken from the other. Blue light gathered in front of Jim's heart and solidified into the metal chest plate a split second before the mace struck it—just like it had once done during Jim's first battle with Bular. As before, the collision of enchanted weapon against enchanted armor sent Jim rocketing high into the night sky.

"Jim!" screamed Claire as Jim flew out of the ransacked village.

Blinky and AAARRRGGHH!!! struggled against the carbon-copy Tellad-Urrs, but to no avail. Suddenly reinvigorated with rage, Claire willed her staff to open a small portal and said, "Don't worry, I'll catch him!"

Admiring the Shadow Staff's abilities, Tellad-Urr tore it from Claire's hand, then tossed her into the shrinking portal. The last thing Claire saw was the dark Trollhunter's face—now screwed into a mask of absolute rancor—before the opening closed and her body hurtled aimlessly into unyielding darkness.

CHAPTER 6
MAZES & MONSTERS

The Creepslayerz had stopped screaming again—but that was only because they were too busy running for their lives.

"I wish I never met stupid Lake and stumbled into his stupid secret life!" said Steve, looking back at the enraged Trolls in hot pursuit behind him.

"Ahh! Don't eat me!" squealed Eli when NotEnrique jumped onto him.

"Relax! I'm not gonna eat ya," assured NotEnrique. "I just wanted a front-row seat when Kilfred's posse does!"

Following their black-and-white leader, the Troll mob knocked over more boxes of salvaged goods and gained on their human quarry. Steve poured on more speed, but Eli struggled to keep up with his more athletic classmate—especially with a laughing Changeling clinging to his shirttails like a demented rodeo clown. To Eli, it felt as if the Trolls were hounding them through a labyrinth of crates. It reminded him of the Minotaurs from the role-playing game his mom bought for him, Mazes & Monsters. Eli's eyes then went wide behind his glasses when he remembered another of his mom's gifts. He jumped in the air and clicked his heels together, causing roller skate wheels to pop out of the soles of his sneakers.

"Zip-Slippers are a GO!" said Eli as he began coasting along the warehouse floor.

"'Zip-Slippers'?" NotEnrique cracked up again.

Ignoring the Changeling's sniggering, Eli looked over his shoulder and smiled. With each skate of his feet, he put more and more distance between himself and Kilfred's chasing Trolls. Satisfied, Eli looked ahead again, just in time to see his body collide with Steve's.

"Watch it, weirdo!" said Steve as he tangled with Eli and fell to the ground.

"Sorry!" Eli squeaked, his wheeled feet slipping and sliding uncontrollably.

"Strike now!" Kilfred ordered to his advancing Trolls. "While the little one is dancing!"

Steve looked from the oncoming wave of irate Trolls to Eli, who continued to skate wildly, going nowhere fast with a cackling green munchkin on his head.

"Why does this keep *happening* to us?!" Steve yelled before jumping onto Eli.

The momentum carried them away from the Trolls—Eli skating at the bottom, Steve piggyback-riding on top, and NotEnrique laughing his head off somewhere in the middle.

"You may be doing permanent damage to my spine, but I've never felt so alive!" Eli said.

"If you tell anyone about this, you won't ever feel alive again!" Steve threatened back.

Their bodies moving as one, the Creepslayerz (plus NotEnrique) whizzed between columns of crates, hanging sharp turns at corners and leaving Kilfred's crew in their dust. Now out of the Trolls' line of sight, Steve indicated an open crate dead ahead, its front panel angled on the floor in front of it like a ramp. Eli nodded and scooted the three of them right up the panel and into the large wooden box. Steve reached back and shut the crate with them inside of it a split second before Kilfred and the Trolls ran past them.

Fumbling in the darkness, Steve pulled out his phone. The home screen lit up the entire inside of the crate, revealing Eli's face an inch away from Steve's. Startled, he dropped his phone with a clatter, which echoed loudly inside their box.

"Shh!" Eli whispered urgently.

"No, *you* shh!" Steve whispered back.

NotEnrique chuckled at the bickering Creepslayerz, until Steve clamped his hand down on the Changeling's mouth. Eli pressed his ear to the side and heard the Trolls debating nearby.

"Lazy and inept, the lot of you!" said Kilfred's voice. "Why, in my day, we'd have two fleshbags like that as an appetizer!"

"Apologies, Kilfred," Bagdwella said. "But, you see, we made a pact some time ago not to eat humans. We were so caught up in your return, we must've slipped back into old habits."

Eli pulled out a little pad of paper and marker to take notes, but Steve slapped them away.

"Then my next decree as your leader is to

renegotiate the so-called 'pact,'" Kilfred decided. "Forget those two children who evaded us and take me to this . . . Arcadia."

Steve, Eli, and NotEnrique all traded a look of wide-eyed alarm as they heard the grumbling Trolls vacate the warehouse. Waiting a full minute after the last Troll shuffled outside, the crate opened and the Creepslayerz stumbled out. Eli said, "I think Kilfred just declared World War T on our hometown! The *T* stands for 'Troll,' by the way."

"Yeah, thanks for connecting the dots on that one, Eli," Steve said sarcastically.

"This is bad news," added NotEnrique, not laughing anymore. "Even by Troll standards."

"So what do we do?" Steve demanded. "Lake normally handles this stuff, right? But he's probably relaxing in some ancient Egyptian hot tub with dragons and other extinct animals!"

Eli was about to correct *several* of the things Steve just said, when something caught his eye. Adjusting his glasses, he peered back into their crate and said, "Whoa, check this out. . . ."

Steve looked over Eli's shoulder and saw a treasure trove of Troll supplies.

"Guess we were too busy not getting eaten to notice this junk," said Steve.

"This isn't junk," Eli continued. "You said it earlier: Jim would normally save the day, only he isn't here. That means it's up to *us*. But we can't go out there unarmed. So, from one protector of the night to another, I ask you: How will we answer fate's urgent distress call?"

"Action-movie lock-and-load montage!" said the Creepslayerz in unison.

Steve and Eli jumped into the crate and mined its contents for usable items. They stuffed their pockets with rounded crystals that looked just like their smoke bombs. They tore strips of red fabric from a Troll flag and wore them as headbands. They tucked rusted swords through their belts and drew patterns on their faces like war paint.

After a few minutes of intense preparation, the Creepslayerz emerged armed to the teeth. Steve and Eli nodding approvingly at each other, their chests puffed with pride, their minds ready for battle. NotEnrique took one look at them—and howled with laughter. He pounded his fists on the concrete floor, laughing so hard he was crying.

"Look at you!" NotEnrique gasped between giggles. "Look at yer little outfits!"

Steve and Eli self-consciously dropped their heroic poses. After a solid minute of tittering, the little Changeling wiped his eyes and said, "But seriously, you twerps are in way over yer heads. I'd better call in a few favors before Kilfred's invasion gets even more outta hand. You two stay here and stay outta trouble!"

As soon as NotEnrique scampered out of the warehouse and into the woods, Steve turned to Eli and asked, "He doesn't really think we're gonna listen to him, does he?"

"And miss out on all the fun?" Eli answered with a knowing wink.

They performed an elaborate secret handshake with lots of slaps, bumps, and finger snaps before Steve ran for the exit and yelled, "Creepslayerz—HO!"

Eli started to follow him, but skidded his Zip-Slippers to a halt in front of another open crate. It contained several tiny carved totems, each them attached to a loop of string.

"Neat-o," said Eli as he pocketed one of the Troll necklaces and skated after his pal.

CHAPTER 7
LOST AND FOUND AND LOST AGAIN

Claire tried to stay calm as she careened uncontrollably through the Shadow Realm.

Although she regularly traveled this dimension whenever teleporting from one portal to another, Claire never liked to spend more time here than absolutely necessary. The inky black abyss always set her nerves on edge, as if she were being constantly watched by the darkness itself. Even now, Claire's body ached, her skull throbbed.

A floating island of lifeless gray rock tumbled past Claire. Working through her illness, she grabbed on to the slow-moving asteroid to steady herself. Claire shut her eyes to stop the dizziness in her head. The vertigo faded—only to be replaced by something worse.

Poor darling fawn, a cold, distant voice spoke in Claire's mind. *Poor little girl lost.*

Claire's eyes snapped open. She looked around the unmoored island, only to find herself alone.

Open a big enough door, something's bound to escape, the voice returned.

Claire then heard the faint echo of an icy laugh over the rushing blood in her ears. Searching for its source, Claire spotted a speck of light twinkling against the infinite shadows.

The other portal! Claire realized.

She kicked off the asteroid toward the light. Like a skydiver, Claire pulled her arms tight against her torso and pressed her legs together to cut down on resistance. Building speed, she arrowed toward the portal and now understood what had happened to her. When Tellad-Urr took the Shadow Staff, he closed the entrance portal behind Claire, trapping her in the Shadow Realm. But she had also opened a *second* portal—an exit—which still remained open, thanks to Claire's emotional anchor.

"Jim!" Claire cried as she saw his limp body plummet past the other side of the portal.

Streamlining herself even more, Claire flew

through the portal, leaving the Shadow Realm and entering the predawn sky high above the moorlands. As gravity once again reclaimed her, bracing gusts buffeted Claire's body, whipping her silver-streaked hair into her face. Clearing her eyes, Claire saw Jim's unconscious body falling below her own. She dove after him and wrapped her arms around his armored chest so that they fell together.

"Wha— Claire?!" Jim roused, surprised by her sudden appearance.

"Told ya I'd catch ya," Claire yelled.

"Thanks! But who's gonna catch us?" Jim asked.

He and Claire looked down at the oncoming ground. Jim figured they were less than half a minute away from splattering against the moors, which actually looked quite lovely from this height. Twisting in the air, Jim put his body between Claire and the earth and said, "Hold on!"

"I appreciate the gesture, but chivalry isn't gonna help us now!" Claire said.

Scant seconds from impact, Jim touched the flickering Amulet on his chest and said, "It will if this baby's got enough juice left to protect us from one! Last! Punch!"

Jim and Claire intertwined their fingers just before their bodies slammed into a shallow river bisecting the moors. Reacting a heartbeat prior to the plunge, the Amulet used the last of its borrowed energy to generate a force field around the two teens. The magical shell insulated them against the full effects of the impact, then shattered into oblivion.

At once, Jim felt the chest plate dissolve and the shock of the cold river water against his body. He grabbed his Amulet before it sank, and Claire grabbed Jim, frantically pulling them both to the surface. Their heads burst out of the river, gasping for air. Grateful to be alive, Jim and Claire embraced, then paddled for the shore. They dragged their sodden bodies onto the marshy bank, next to a small stone footbridge that crossed the river.

"I always wanted to visit England," said Claire. "But not like this."

Jim shivered miserably beside her, adding, "And I thought I was homesick in the Darklands. At least you're feeling well enough to shadow-jump again."

"N-not that it matters now," Claire replied through chattering teeth. "That Tellad-Urr clone stole my staff before he punted me into the Shadow Realm. I don't know how we're going to get back to Toby, Blinky, and AAARRRGGHH!!!"

Jim heard the rumble of plodding footsteps approach the river. Clambering up the sandy bank, he looked out at the moors, and his eyes immediately bulged in alarm.

"Actually, I think they're coming to us," Jim said as he slid down the river bank, took Claire by the arm, and pulled her under the footbridge.

The stone arch sprinkled silt onto their heads as five Tellad-Urr the Terribles marched above them. Keeping absolutely still, Jim and Claire looked over to the river's waters, which reflected the grim army above them. One of the dark Trollhunters hefted the Sundown Mace, three pushed the covered wheelbarrows full of "tributes," and the last held a fistful of chains. Jim and Claire's hearts sank as they saw the rippling reflections of Toby, Blinky, and AAARRRGGHH!!!—each of them shackled and pulled along as Tellad-Urr's prisoners.

"Tellad-Urr, I implore you to listen to reason," said Blinky, rattling the cuffs on all four of his hands. "We are all Trolls here. Surely we can come to some sort of peaceful solution."

"Well, technically, I'm not a Troll," Toby stipulated. "But I was crowned king of the Quagawumps for an hour. We even came up with a dance in my honor!"

"A peaceful solution," Tellad-Urr snorted derisively. "Do you have any idea how often I pleaded to Merlin for peace? For even the slightest reprieve from his Amulet's constant demands?"

As they crossed the footbridge, one of the wheelbarrows hit a raised cobblestone, causing it to spill. Jim and Claire heard its contents fall over the bridge and tinkle against the river stones beside them. Picking up one the scraps, Jim recognized it as an iron fastener that once rested on that village's front gate. Even in the absence of light under the bridge, he saw that the metal had been wrenched out of place. It now appeared as twisted and bent as the Trollhunter above them.

"I knew no peace as a champion," said Tellad-Urr the Terrible, ignoring the imminent sunrise. "So why should it be any different for the worlds I was duped into protecting?"

Jim shook the water out of his Amulet and

whispered to Claire, "I need to help them."

"No!" Claire whispered back. "You can't help them if you're dead!"

"We can't just leave the guys with that red lunatic—" Jim quietly protested.

"You really think Tellad-Urr'll let you pirate more of his Amulet's magic?" Claire breathed. "We need a plan first. You know that's what Blinky would say."

Jim looked into Claire's eyes and knew she was right. He let out a weary sigh, which was drowned out by the last of the Tellad-Urrs' footsteps as they cleared the bridge.

"We'll get 'em back, Jim," Claire promised as their friends disappeared over the next hill.

"Even if I *can* find a way to rescue Tobes and Blink and AAARRRGGHH!!!, how am I supposed to return us all to our own time?" Jim said out loud now that they were alone. "My Amulet's still on the fritz, and I don't even know what year I'm in!"

"On the human calendar or the Troll calendar?" someone asked.

Jim and Claire slowly turned and discovered a River Troll staring at them from the shadow of the bridge. The Troll took a step forward, causing Jim and Claire to scream. But their scream made the Troll scream in response. Jim and Claire looked at each other as the River Troll backed away meekly.

"Um, I'm guessing you're not a fan of Tellad-Urr either," said Jim, watching how the Troll's knees knocked in fright.

"Are you crazy?" the River Troll replied. "I've been hiding under here for three weeks just to avoid that one-horned tyrant!"

"Then we're on the same side," said Claire, recovering from her initial shock. "I'm Claire and this is Jim, the Trollhunter—"

The Troll screamed again.

"No, no! He's a good one! From . . . from far away!" Claire quickly added.

The River Troll studied the two humans for a beat before he slowly crept toward them. The sky lightened over the bridge, letting Jim and Claire get a better look at him. The Troll appeared frail and old, the patches of moss on his body having faded from green to gray long ago. He wore a burlap smock, and even the horns on the boulder atop his head bent downward, as if they, too, had grown weak in age.

"Pleased to meet you," said the River Troll. "The name's Gogun."

Jim and Claire's eyes bugged in amazement. With a jubilant whoop, they grabbed each other's arms and began jumping for joy under the bridge. The old Troll scowled at the noise.

"We found Gogun the Gentle!" Claire cheered.

"I'm Gogun the *Graceful*," Gogun griped in annoyance. "You must have me confused with someone else."

Jim and Claire stopped jumping.

"It's probably a coincidence," Gogun continued. "In my generation, 'Gogun' is a pretty popular Troll name. It's right up there with 'Shmorkrarg.'"

"But . . . there are no coincidences in Trollhunting," Jim said. "Only destiny."

"Is that so? Well, my destiny is to stay under this bridge until I croak from old age or Tellad-Urr destroys the world—whichever comes first," Gogun announced with some finality.

Jim shook his head, pressed his defective Amulet into the old Troll's hands, and said, "Listen, I know this is going to sound crazy. And that's because it *is* crazy. And you can call yourself whatever you want, Gogun, but this Amulet brought us here for a reason. Claire and I, we need your help. To find our friends. To free them. To stop Tellad-Urr once and for all so his Amulet can pass onto yo—the next Trollhunter."

Claire patted her boyfriend on the back, proud of his speech. Jim smiled, seeing his words stir deep feelings within the Troll.

"Are you insane?" shrieked Gogun. "Me? Fight Tellad-Urr? The Terrible?"

"It's the only way you can become the next Trollhunter," Claire explained patiently.

"But I don't *wanna* be a Trollhunter!" Gogun yelled, then broke into a sob. "I've spent my whole life running from conflict! That, and those tiny, bald, drooling surface creatures."

Jim gaped in confusion before asking, "Are . . . are you talking about *babies*?"

Gogun screamed again at the very mention of them. Claire leaned closer to Jim and asked, "How's an old Troll who's afraid of babies going to become Merlin's next champion?"

Jim winced, coming to the conclusion that he'd never cook dinner for his mom again.

CHAPTER 8
BATTLEFIELD ARCADIA

Steve saw the moonlit edge of the woods just ahead and said, "We're getting closer."

"Aw, I'm glad you feel that way too, Steve," said Eli with a happy smile. "The greatest weapon in the Creepslayerz' arsenal is our friendship!"

"What?" said Steve.

"Who'd have thought?" Eli continued, unaware of the disgust on Steve's face. "One day you're shoving me into a locker, the next you're—"

Steve pushed Eli off the path and into some shrubs.

"—shoving me into poison ivy," Eli mumbled as he got to his feet and rejoined Steve.

Stopping at the tree line, they crouched low and peered between two oaks. They saw Arcadia Oaks'

Main Street just beyond them—and Kilfred's Troll parade walking right toward it. The lampposts lit up their bulky stone bodies as they passed the various shops and restaurants, studying their own curious reflections in the windows. Fortunately, the Trolls had arrived after hours, and everything was closed with no human residents in sight.

"For once, I'm glad this loser town doesn't have a nightlife scene," Steve muttered.

"You're right," said Eli. "Yes, most of our neighbors are asleep right now, but someone's bound to notice Kilfred's search-and-destroy party sooner or later. Unless . . ."

"'Unless' what?" Steve asked.

"Unless we can convince the Trolls that Arcadia is so dangerous, they'd be better off back in the warehouse," Eli mused. "It's a classic smoke-and-mirrors campaign."

"Then it's a good thing I brought the smoke," Steve said with a grin as he held up the rounded crystals he took from the Troll crate.

"Smoke bombs," said Eli in hushed awe, recognizing the similarity they bore to the ones his mom bought from the magic shop.

The Creepslayerz ninja-ed out of the woods and over to Main Street. They stopped every now and then to duck behind a statue or drop and roll onto the ground like commandos—even though the Trolls weren't even looking in their direction.

"Look at these crass, pointless edifices the fleshbags have built," Steve and Eli heard Kilfred say from their current location behind a park bench. "Since when do mighty Trolls cower from a species that needs to purchase its magic from a shop?"

The Creepslayerz peeked long enough to see the other Trolls mutter in agreement with Kilfred's sentiments. Some started knocking over public trash cans, punching mailboxes, and rocking the parked cars, setting off their theft alarms.

"It's now or never," said Eli. "Let's go!"

"This is for the graduating class of Arcadia Oaks High!" Steve shouted. "GO MOLES!"

With that, Steve called upon his years of baseball practice and threw the smoke bombs at the Trolls.

A massive fireball mushroomed into the night air, setting off any remaining car alarms that the Trolls had not yet triggered. The force of the explosion knocked Steve off his feet and sent Eli tumbling after him. They landed in the park adjacent to Main Street, their ears ringing and faces blackened with soot. Unharmed by the blast, the assembled Trolls retreated from the blazing remains of Alex's Arcade and whipped into an even greater frenzy than before.

"Do you see?" hollered Kilfred, pointing at the inferno behind him. "The fleshbags fear our superiority, so they now seek to attack us! Must we Trolls suffer again at their mad whims? It's time for us to retaliate in kind!"

The black-and-white Troll led his followers on a tear away from Main Street and into Arcadia Oaks at large.

"I don't think that was a smoke bomb," reasoned Eli.

"Nah, it was a Dwärkstone grenade, ya dorks," sniped a familiar voice behind them.

Steve and Eli turned and discovered NotEnrique, flanked on either side by Walter Strickler and Ms. Nomura. The green imp shook his head and added, "Toldja you was in way over yer heads."

CHAPTER 9
NOT-SO-GREAT GRONKA MORKA

Blinky's homecoming to his childhood Trollmarket would've been a lot more special without the handcuffs.

Tellad-Urr's doppelgangers had dragged him, AAARRRGGHH!!!, Toby, and their wheelbarrows full of metal for what felt like miles across the English moors. Just before the sun rose, they reached the tall hill known as Glastonbury Tor, where the dark Trollhunter drew open a Horngazel passage. Blinky had squinted his many eyes as he and his two friends were pressed through the blinding tunnel of light and rock. Once they reached the other side, Blinky's vision returned, and he beheld the Trollmarket in which he had grown up. It now seemed much smaller to the adult Blinky, although he easily recognized the purple Heartstone growing upside down from the cavern ceiling. Below that, he saw the many caves he had frequented as a young Troll, yet they now seemed to be without occupants. In fact, most of Glastonbury Tor Trollmarket appeared devoid of much life or warmth at all to Blinky.

"This way, six-eyed scum," ordered the Tellad-Urr holding Blinky's chain.

Blinky stumbled alongside AAARRRGGHH!!! and Toby as two of the dark Trollhunter duplicates led them lower, while the rest wheeled away the barrows. Toby tugged the abrasive shackle around his neck and said, "Not too big on hospitality in the Dark Ages, are they?"

"Indeed," Blinky seconded. "I remember every Troll here being rather pleasant—except my older brother, Dictatious. He always was an insufferable, egotistical, opportunistic—"

"Jerk," AAARRRGGHH!!! finished, ducking his mossy green head as they were prodded into the cramped confines of the Trollmarket's dungeon.

The three prisoners' hearts sank as they took in the dank warren of caves, each barred by a web of orange crystal spikes. The only sounds they heard were the trickle of foul-smelling water along the mold-slicked walls and the defeated moans of more captured Trolls. One of the Tellad-Urrs inserted an oversized key into the dungeon wall, causing the orange spikes to retract. The second shoved Toby, Blinky, and AAARRRGGHH!!! into the now-open cell.

"Say, uh, mister unicorn Troll, sir?" Toby said politely. "Would you mind giving me back my Warhammer? It has sentimental value."

"One of my others has buried it at the bottom of my vault," answered the Tellad-Urr. "Just as you will soon fill the bottom of my belly!"

The identical Trollhunters barked in laughter and removed the key. With a hiss, the crystal spikes slid back into place, sealing Toby, Blinky, and AAARRRGGHH!!! into the dungeon. Still cackling, the Tellad-Urrs left, taking the only key with them.

"It was worth a try," Toby mumbled, before something brushed against him in the dark.

Toby yelped and hid behind his massive wing-man. Being a Krubera, AAARRRGGHH!!! was accustomed to the low-light conditions of Earth's deepest caves and, therefore, was the first to spot their cellmates. Toby and Blinky's eyes soon adjusted too, and saw scores of withered Trolls shambling toward them. Their stone skin sallow and their eyes protruding with hunger, they closed in around Toby, Blinky, and AAARRRGGHH!!!

"Oh, great!" Toby cried. "I suppose all you old-school Trolls want to eat me too!"

The imprisoned Trolls halted in place, looking insulted. One said, "Eat you? Why would we ever want to do that? You look disgusting."

"Whew! Thanks!" Toby whistled in relief, before the rest sunk in. "I think?"

Blinky inspected the wilting Trolls and said, "They're being deprived of the Heartstone's nourishing glow in this dungeon."

"Made weak...on purpose," said AAARRRGGHH!!!

"You mean . . . this'll happen to both of you the longer we stay down here?" Toby asked, casting a concerned look over his two friends. "We've gotta bust outta here *pronto*!"

"Agreed, but not just yet," Blinky said before addressing the sickly Trolls. "I say, what has brought all of you to this dismal place? You certainly don't *seem* like criminals."

"We're not," wheezed a prisoner. "Unless you count 'refusing to attack fleshlings' as a crime.

Tellad-Urr certainly does. . . ."

"You mean . . . the dark Trollhunter demands you eat humans?" Blinky inquired, aghast.

"No, Kilfred had more of a taste for that . . . though Gorgus knows where he and his lackeys have disappeared to," answered another captive. "Tellad-Urr the Terrible doesn't care whether we eat humans or not. He just wants us to raid their villages for his 'tributes.'"

"Those wheelbarrows full of metal," said Blinky. "But what would Merlin's misguided champion need with all that worthless pig iron?"

"Maybe he's practicing Troll dentistry?" Toby guessed, his braces twinkling.

All six of Blinky's eyes focused on his young teammate's metal mouth, then brightened with an idea. "Tobias, have I complimented you on your smile lately? Why, it lights up this very dungeon— and may provide our means of escape from it."

Toby grinned wider, allowing Blinky to reach inside and pluck the wire from his braces.

"Ow!" cried Toby.

"My apologies, but we have to move quickly if this is going to work," Blinky said, reeling a seemingly endless strand of wire from Toby's braces. "AAARRRGGHH!!!, I believe now's a suitable time to make yourself comfortable."

AAARRRGGHH!!! broke all his chains with a casual shrug. The shattered restraints fell to the floor with a clatter, making the imprisoned Trolls around him perk up in hope.

"Wha—?!" Toby gasped as Blinky finished unspooling the last bit of wire. "You mean, you could've broken free at any time? Why the heck didn't you do that earlier?"

"I advised him not to, as soon as those facsimile Tellad-Urrs tackled us in that village," said Blinky, now bending the enormous bale of wire this way and that with his many hands.

AAARRRGGHH!!! snapped the chains off Toby and Blinky, who completed tweaking the wire. Its new shape reminded Toby of a giant circuit—and of the weird key held by their one-horned jailer. Blinky carefully threaded the kinked dental wire past the crystal spikes and hooked it into the dungeon's keyhole.

"Besides, I'd like a closer look at that vault Tellad-Urr mentioned," Blinky continued, gingerly probing with the wire. "If memory serves, it's full of useful bric-a-brac, including—"

"A Kairosect! Yes!" exclaimed Toby, catching on.

"Clonk-donk home," AAARRRGGHH!!! added as he unshackled the remaining Trolls.

"Just so," Blinky affirmed, wrenching the wire in a sudden counterclockwise motion.

A satisfying clack echoed from the lock tumblers embedded in the dungeon, and the crystal spikes sank back into the walls. Blinky gestured to the way out and said, "Voilà!"

"Nice to see thousands of dollars of orthodontic hardware finally pay off!" Toby quipped. "Although if I told Dr. Muelas about any of this, he'd think it was the laughing gas talking. . . ."

Impressed by Blinky's ingenuity, the freed Trolls all dropped to their knees and bowed to their savior. Surprised by the sudden genuflection, Blinky said, "Great Gronka Morka!"

"Great Gronka Morka!" repeated the worshipping Trolls. "Great Gronka Morka!"

Blinky, Toby, and AAARRRGGHH!!! all looked to each other in surprise before the six-eyed Troll said, "I-I thank you for your praise, but please stop. My name is actually Bl—"

"Great Gronka Morka! Great Gronka Morka!" chanted the liberated Trolls.

"No, no, no," Blinky dismissed impatiently. "Great Gronka Morka was a legendary wise Troll. A scholar, much like myself, with six eyes, also much like myself, who appeared out of the blue one day to lead one of the most famous jailbreaks in Troll legend and—"

Blinky's six eyes shot wide open with sudden realization. He slapped all four of his hands against his skull and cried, "Oh my Gorgus—*I'm* Great Gronka Morka!"

"Great Gronka Morka! Great Gronka Morka! Great Gronka Morka!" the Trolls resumed.

"Confusing," admitted AAARRRGGHH!!! with a shake of his head.

"You mean, all this time you've been saying your own name every time you're freaked out by something?" Toby asked. "Maybe I should try that. *Holy Toby!*"

"What have I done?" Blinky muttered as the line of thankful Trolls hugged him on the way out of dungeon. "I only pray Master Jim and Claire are unharmed and doing their level best to not alter the course of history. . . ."

CHAPTER 10
GOGUN WEPT

"Take it!" Jim yelled, thrusting the Amulet into Gogun's hands for the umpteenth time. "Take it! Take it! Take it!"

The inactive device slipped out of the old Troll's fingers as he broke down sobbing again. Jim threw up his hands in frustration.

"I don't want the Amulet!" Gogun blubbered. "I don't want to be a Trollhunter! I don't want to duh-duh-dieeeeeeee!"

Claire rolled her eyes as Gogun dropped to the soggy ground under the footbridge, crying even harder. She then tapped Jim and suggested, "Maybe we should try a *softer* sell. You've always said how overwhelmed you felt when you first became the Trollhunter."

"My situation hasn't exactly improved since then," Jim deadpanned over more wails.

"There you go," said Claire. "This is a big responsibility you're asking Gogun to accept. Maybe try telling him something that comforted you when you were in his place."

"Right," Jim replied, thinking it over.

Stuffing his hands in his pockets, Jim approached the old Troll, who still sobbed in the river muck, and said, "Hey, uh, Gogun."

Gogun uncurled from the fetal position and, in a voice thick with tears, said, "What?"

"I know being the Trollhunter is kind of a heavy destiny," Jim started. "But someone once told me that destiny is a gift."

"It . . . it is?" sniffled Gogun.

"Yeah!" said Jim, encouraged by Gogun's interest. "See, some go their entire lives living an existence of quiet desperation, never learning the truth. That what feels like a burden pushing down upon our shoulders is actually the sense of purpose that lifts us to greater heights."

"'Greater . . . greater heights'?" echoed Gogun, now wiping the tears from his cheeks.

"Never forget that fear is but the precursor to valor. That to strive and triumph in the face of fear is what it means to be a hero," Jim's voice swelled. "Don't think. Become."

The old Troll's lips moved as he silently mouthed the last part of the speech. Gogun then stood up tall, wiped the slop from his body, and said, "Become what? A *corpse*?!"

"What? No!" said Jim as Gogun retreated.

"That's not what he was saying at all!" vouched Claire.

"I told you," Gogun said, his voice rising in anger. "I don't want to—"

"Be the Trollhunter, yeah, yeah, yeah," Jim finished for him. "Pretty sure I heard you the first hundred times. Fine. So what *do* you want then?"

"Nobody . . . nobody's ever asked me that," Gogun said, his pique fading. "But if I had a choice in the matter, I suppose I want to do what I've always felt I was born to do."

"And what's that?" said Claire, genuinely intrigued.

Gogun held his hands by his face, wiggled his fingers enthusiastically, and said, "Dance!"

Jim and Claire watched the old Troll in bafflement. He started kicking his feet in rhythm, splashing the water and twirling his body as he hummed to himself.

"At least now we know why he goes by 'the Graceful,'" reasoned Claire just before Gogun tripped and fell face-first into the river.

"We are so doomed," said Jim.

Claire doubled over with a coughing fit. Jim ran to her side, but she waved him off, saying, "I'll . . . I'll be all right."

"I know when you're acting, Nuñez," Jim replied. "You're getting sicker the longer we stay here. We gotta get back to our own time. To actual medicine, not leeches and bloodletting."

"That . . . that might be a while," Claire said hoarsely.

Jim felt a renewed pang of worry as he watched Claire ease herself down to the bank, cup her hands into the river, and drink its waters. Gogun sidled up beside Jim, dripping on him.

"You . . . care for her, don't you?" asked the Troll, following Jim's line of sight to Claire.

"Yeah," Jim acknowledged. "I do."

"Yes, I can remember what it was like to feel that way for another," sighed Gogun wistfully, his eyes distant with the onset of memory. "She was called . . . Shmorkrarg."

Jim blinked in puzzlement before the old Troll said, "I told you it was a common name. Although everything else about her—her beauty, her fiery passion—was most uncommon. My Shmorkrarg had this funny little way of breaking boulders against her skull. And whenever she smote an enemy, she'd get the most alluring look in her one eye. . . ."

"Sounds . . . special," Jim mumbled wearily.

Gogun sighed, shook the nostalgia from his head, and pulled an unassuming plant from the riverbank. He handed the green shoot to Jim and said, "Here. Succor root. This should help your unfortunate-looking ladyfriend with her cough."

Jim felt his spirits rise as he looked from the sprout to Claire and back to Gogun. The ancient, sopping-wet Troll picked up the discarded Amulet from the shoals. He breathed in heavy acceptance, then said, "It's certainly beautiful." Then he moved his hand up and down a bit and added, "It's heavier than it looks. Now tell me . . . does this thing come with instructions?"

Jim cracked a smile and said, "You're looking at them."

"Again," Jim called as the midday light dappled through the trees.

He and Claire watched Gogun practice sword fighting with a stick in the forest to which they had moved. The Troll kept to the shade, thrusting, parrying, and striking with his branch.

"Gettin' better, Gogun!" Claire encouraged from the sidelines.

Gogun lowered the branch and took a bow, but lost his balance and fell over once more.

Jim covered his face with his hand and said, "Again."

Golden rays of late-afternoon sunlight filtered into the forest as Jim and Gogun now sparred with two sticks. Jim intentionally moved slower than normal, allowing the elderly Troll to deflect each pretend blow.

"Good," Jim said. "Just make sure to watch your

flanks. Gumm-Gumms love to stab their enemies in the back."

Proud of himself, Gogun held the branch sideways like a cane and started tap-dancing in the middle of the forest. Claire clapped along, until Jim shot her a dirty look.

"How many times do I have to tell you? *Please* stop dancing," Jim said, covering his face anew. "And again."

With the sunset now reddening the sky over the forest, Jim and Claire watched Gogun successfully complete an attack/defense combo, roll forward on the leafy ground, and plant his sword-stick into a log that sort of looked like a dead Gumm-Gumm.

"Awesomesauce!" Jim and Claire applauded together.

Slightly out of breath, Gogun said, "You know, you're not a bad teacher, Kim."

Claire snorted, but quickly recovered when she saw Jim glowering at her.

"I'm not laughing," she fibbed. "That was a sneeze. *Ah-choo* again."

"My. Name. Is. Jim," Jim said to Gogun between clenched teeth.

"Really?" Gogun said, legitimately surprised. "I thought I heard you say 'Kim.'"

"*Jim,*" Jim repeated through his grinding jaws.

"Oh. Well. Sorry." Gogun shrugged. "Either way, I think we can stop training now."

He looked sideways and saw an unconvinced Jim glaring back at him. So Gogun flexed his arms like a body builder and started strutting around the forest with feigned confidence. He then added, "Yeah, I've, uh, never felt so lethal. And thanks to you, I now appreciate the, er, sacred obligation of the Trollhunter and solemnly swear to uphold and—oooh, kitties!"

Jim and Claire watched slack-jawed as Gogun ran over to a bush and cradled the litter of kittens that had just pounced out of it. He scratched behind their furry little ears with the tip of his stone finger and nuzzled their purring bellies with his nose.

"Hewwo, dere!" Gogun baby-talked to the cats. "Who's a cute widdle kitten? You are!"

"I thought Trolls ate cats," Claire finally said, still wrapping her head around the sight.

"And humans," Gogun said with a bitter edge.

"Guess I'm not like other Trolls, hmm?"

"No. No, you're not," Jim said with mounting annoyance.

"I'm going to name you 'Shmorkrarg,'" Gogun told one of the kittens. "Oh yes, I am!"

Claire looked at the dusk and said, "If we're going to make our move, it's now or never."

"Right," Jim replied as the future Trollhunter rolled on the ground with the kittens. "C'mon, Gogun. Time for some on-the-job training."

By the light of the rising moon, Jim, Claire, and Gogun followed the gargantuan footprints left by all five Tellad-Urr the Terribles to a towering hill.

"Glastonbury Tor," Jim said as they reached the summit and looked around.

"Never much cared for Glastonberries, I don't mind telling you," Gogun commented with a sour face. "Too tart for my tastes."

"Thanks for that information," snarked Jim. "Super helpful."

Claire elbowed Jim's side and cocked her head in a clear gesture toward Gogun. *Be nice.* Jim massaged his ribs, then moved over to a cluster of monolithic boulders at the top of the Tor.

"This must be where they Horngazel in and out of their Trollmarket," Jim said, pressing his palms against the smooth rock. "I guess we just have to wait for a new portal to open and—"

Jim cut off when he heard a distinct *meow* from the other side of the boulder. Craning his head around it, he saw Gogun sitting cross-legged on the hill, playing with the kittens that were now crawling out of his smock.

"You brought them with you?!" Jim yelled.

"Uh, *yeah*," Gogun replied, as if it were the most logical thing in the world. "I mean, you try looking into Shmorkrarg's fuzzy little face and telling her no. It's not so easy!"

"She is pretty cute," Claire admitted before a strange sense of foreboding overtook her body. "Everybody hide. Now!"

Jim jumped behind the boulder alongside Claire, Gogun, and the kittens as the atmosphere around Glastonbury Tor darkened. They peered around the side and saw a portal manifest out of thin air.

"That doesn't look like any Horngazel passage I've ever seen," said Jim.

"That's because it's not," Claire said. "I don't know how, but I can feel it in my bones—that's a shadow portal!"

Jim, Claire, and Gogun ducked once more as a black hole dilated on the other side of the boulder. Thunder rumbled, and Tellad-Urr the Terrible emerged, clutching the Shadow Staff.

"Oh no," Jim said, his voice below a whisper. "How can this day get any worse?"

Lightning flashed in the sky, illuminating two other Trolls who now climbed the opposite end of the hill and joined Tellad-Urr. Jim's and Claire's faces drained of color as they recognized the hunched newcomers in the next strobe of lightning.

"You were supposed to be alone," said Tellad-Urr to the largest of the two figures. "That was our arrangement."

"*I* dictate the terms, Terrible One," replied Gunmar the Black. "Now watch your tone. I won't suffer any who speak with such disrespect to me—or my heir."

The sky flashed again, revealing in full the horrible visages of the Gumm-Gumm general and his wild-eyed son, Bular.

CHAPTER 11
DORKSTONE GRENADES

"Well, well, well," said Strickler with a disappointed *tsk*. "Why am I not surprised?"

He, Nomura, and NotEnrique looked upon Steve and Eli as Main Street went up in flames around them. The Creepslayerz clutched each other on the park lawn, and Eli stuttered, "A-a-aren't you the nice lady who works at the history museum?"

"And so much more," Nomura purred. "But you'd better hand over any other Troll contra-band before you inadvertently blow *it* up, too."

The wail of oncoming sirens drowned out the last of her words. The Arcadia Oaks Police and Fire Departments arrived in a hurry, parking their cars and engines haphazardly along Main Street. Strickler's eyes narrowed when they spied Detective

Scott emerge from one of the squad cars.

"You were right to contact us," Strickler said to NotEnrique. "You and Nomura stay here with young Steven and Elijah while I handle Detective Scott. The last thing we need right now is someone tracing this fiasco back to the warehouse."

"*You're* going to talk to the cops?" groused Steve. "But you're . . . you're . . ."

"Still an upstanding, law-abiding citizen of Arcadia Oaks, as far as anyone else knows," Strickler finished, his eyes flashing yellow before reverting to a more human appearance.

Stunned by their former teacher's peepers, the Creepslayerz watched Strickler trot over to Detective Scott—until NotEnrique slapped both of them along the backs of their heads.

"You heard 'im," said the green imp. "Turn out yer pockets, cosplayers."

"That's *Creepslayerz*—with a *z*," Steve insisted.

He and Eli grudgingly handed over everything they had taken from RotGut's crates. NotEnrique rummaged through the small mountain of "borrowed" Troll goods, taking inventory.

"Let's see here," said NotEnrique. "We got four

old, dirty, rusted swords—"

"Greco-Roman *spathas*," Nomura corrected.

"One Horngazel key," NotEnrique continued. "One Glamour Mask—"

"What's that do?" Steve interrupted, pointing at the odd, Tiki-like Troll mask.

"Changes yer appearance," said NotEnrique. "If yer not lucky enough to be a natural-born shape-shifter like yours truly. And it's a good thing ya didn't break it. I went through a *lot* of trouble to find that thing!"

Steve looked back at the firefighters hosing down Alex's Arcade. Beside them, he saw Strickler having a friendly chat with Detective Scott. Steve thought he overheard mention of a "gas main leak" before they shook hands, and Strickler returned to the relative privacy of the park.

"Did they fall for the 'gas main leak' bit?" asked Nomura.

"Hook, line, and *Strickler*," smirked Strickler. "That excuse is an oldie, but a goodie. Now we just have to find a way to return Kilfred and his gaggle of irate Trolls back to the warehouse. But I fear nothing short of Gunmar himself will scare them back into hiding. They are fearless right now."

NotEnrique fixed a suspicious look at the Creepslayerz and asked, "You two got anything else tucked away in yer undies?"

"Just this cool necklace I found," said Eli, putting his head through the loop of twine.

The Changelings' eyes bulged in alarm before Strickler shouted, "No, Eli, don't!"

But it was too late. Eli now wore the necklace.

"What's the big deal?" Steve asked NotEnrique.

Eli's eye twitched. Animal noises gurgled from his throat, and his body convulsed.

"That's no mere necklace," Strickler said. "The Grit-Shaka banishes all fear from Trolls in times of war."

"Oh yeah?" said Steve as Eli ran around in hyperactive circles in front of them. "And what's it do to humans?"

As if on cue, Eli stopped moving, his back to the group. They watched in apprehension as he calmly straightened his posture, removed his glasses, and swept back his hair. In one smooth motion, Eli spun on his heels, snapped his fingers, and flashed everyone a wide, debonair smile.

"Eli?" asked Steve.

"Call me 'Romeo,'" Eli said, winking at Miss Nomura.

NotEnrique cracked up again. As Eli strutted over to the pile of confiscated Troll gear and picked up the Horngazel, Steve explained, "Pepper*whack* was up for the lead role in *Romeo and Juliet*, until Lake scored it with that preppy armor of his."

"All right, *Romeo*," said Strickler. "Playtime's over. Put down the Horngazel and remove the Grit-Shaka at once."

"Nah, I don't think so, Walt," Eli retorted. "Someone's gotta stop those Trolls and that someone . . . is Romeo!"

Without warning, Eli gallantly dipped Ms. Nomura and planted a kiss right on her lips.

"Oi!" yelled NotEnrique as Eli grabbed him by the scruff and ran off down Main Street.

"Eli—I mean, Romeo!" Steve called after him. "Where're you going?"

"I'm gonna find that Gunmar guy Walt just mentioned!" Eli shouted before disappearing around the corner with NotEnrique. "And then I'm gonna Pepper*jack* him up!"

CHAPTER 12
HEAVY METAL

"*What* did you just say?" growled Gunmar.

"I said you don't frighten me, Gumm-Gumm," Tellad-Urr sneered. "Nor does your brute of a son."

From their hiding place behind the boulders, Jim, Claire, and Gogun heard Bular snarl and step toward the dark Trollhunter—only for his father to hold him back with a single hand.

"Let me devour him, father!" Bular roared. "I'll crack open his red shell and sup on the quivering marrow inside! Then use his bones as toothpicks to scrape the sinew from my fangs!"

"Your obscene bloodlust fills my black heart with pride, son," said Gunmar. "But I shall be the one to unmake him."

"You'll do nothing of the sort," the scarlet

Trollhunter replied. "Not while I have these."

Tellad-Urr signaled, and more enslaved Trolls slumped out of the black hole carting those wheelbarrows. Only now, Jim noticed, they carried polished weapons, not iron scraps.

"Crafted from human metal, forged in the crystal furnaces of our Trollmarket," Tellad-Urr said. "You should now have enough to arm every member of your uprising. I've held up my end of our bargain, Gunmar. You do the same."

Bular greedily snatched two matching swords—each fitted with a bone hilt—and slashed them through the air. Gogun shivered, hearing the blades sing from behind the boulder.

"Father, I want these," said Bular.

"Keep them," Gunmar said. "May they ever drip with the blood of your enemies."

Claire's eyes focused on the Shadow Staff—*her* Shadow Staff—in Tellad-Urr's grasp, then on the browbeaten Trolls shipping additional weapons back and forth through the portal. She bent close to Jim and whispered, "That's our ticket into their Trollmarket."

"We're gonna have to time this just right," Jim

said back. "Follow me and keep low!"

Before Gogun could protest, Jim shoved him out from behind the boulder. Claire kept close behind, careful to remain out of their enemies' sights. They'd nearly reached the gateway when everyone heard a soft *mew*. Jim's blood ran cold.

"Quiet, Shmorkie!" Gogun whisper-scolded.

The son of Gunmar unsheathed his new swords and began prowling Glastonbury Tor, while his father argued with the dark Trollhunter in the background.

"You still haven't answered to my satisfaction, Gunmar," said Tellad-Urr.

As Bular stalked closer, Jim hurried Claire and Gogun (and the mewling kittens) behind one of the emptied wheelbarrows that had been left off to the side. With chained Trolls passing around them and Bular getting ever nearer, Jim and Claire climbed inside.

"My word is my bond, Tellad-Urr," they heard Gunmar say. "The Gumm-Gumms will depart quietly and without reprisal, and your Trollhunting duties will be at an end—once I have murdered Orlagk and assumed control of his armies, that is."

Gogun tried to crawl in after Jim and Claire but didn't fit. His voice low due to Bular's proximity, Jim said, "You've gotta blend in with the other Trolls and push us into that portal!"

Claire saw the indecision in the elder Troll's eyes and said, "Do it for Shmorkie, Gogun."

Bular loped over to the train of wheelbarrows funneling to and fro, his twin swords glinting in the moonlight, his back turned to the three trespassers.

Mew.

Bular's head whipped around at once. But all he saw was the back of an old, hobbling Troll in a smock disappearing through the black hole.

Gogun didn't stop hyperventilating until well after he had stumbled out of the other end of the shadow portal.

"You did good, Gogun," complimented Jim, his pulse still racing. "Worthy of a Trollh—"

"Don't say it!" Gogun cried.

"Gogun," began Claire, before a new series of hacking coughs derailed her. "Can you show us where our friends might—"

A loud sniffing noise came from just around the corner. Jim stood protectively in front of Claire as a hulking silhouette stepped in front of them.

"Oh no! It's him! He's back for my kitties!" Gogun shrieked. "AAAIIIEEE!!!"

"Not 'AAAIIIEEE!!!,'" said the huge Troll in front of them. "It's 'AAARRRGGHH!!!'"

Jim and Claire broke into relieved smiles as the backlit figure stepped forward, and AAARRRGGHH!!!'s warm face grinned back at them. Blinky and Toby rushed in behind him.

"Master Jim! Claire!" said Blinky, overjoyed.

"You guys made it!" Toby gushed, hugging them as hard as he could.

With everyone so wrapped up in their reunion, they failed to notice Gogun. He collected his kittens back under his smock and tiptoed off to the side.

"Likewise, Tobes!" Jim said. "We thought we were gonna have to rescue you from Tellad-Urr. Only it looks like you're doing fine without us. . . ."

Jim then saw the many freed Trolls gathered behind Blinky, adding, "And like you made some new friends."

"Oh, I wouldn't call them friends, necessarily," said Blinky. "More like acquaintances we met during our brief incarceration. In fact, Master Jim, until today, I don't believe I've ever seen any of these . . . Trolls . . . before . . ."

Blinky's voice trailed off as he spotted two young Trolls wandering between the other released prisoners. Both were boys, both had four arms, and both had six eyes—just like Blinky. The youngest of the two seemed lost, frightened, until his older sibling handed him a book. They turned its pages together, the little one now smiling in reassurance as his big brother taught him how to read.

"Dictatious?" Blinky uttered in recognition, his voice barely audible. "Then that means the younger one is . . . Great Gronka Morka!"

"Great Gronka Morka!" the other Trolls immediately chanted. "Great Gronka Morka!"

"What in the world is that about?" asked Claire.

"Holy Toby, is *that* a long story," sighed Toby.

As the released Trolls continued their mantra, Jim said to his friends, "Guys, there's someone you've gotta meet. Please say 'hello' to Gogun the . . ."

Jim drew everyone's attention to the spot Gogun had occupied, only to find it empty.

"Gone?" Jim finished in surprise, the old dancing Troll nowhere in sight.

CHAPTER 13
WHEREFORE ART THOU, ROMEO?

"Where'd Pepper*jerk* go?" said Steve as he, Strickler, and Nomura searched through the woods by Main Street.

About fifty feet ahead of them, Eli bounded through the trees, keeping NotEnrique in a head-lock. The little Changeling squirmed and said, "Oi! If you don't lemme go, I swear—"

"Do not swear by the moon, for she changes constantly!" Eli quoted before flipping gracefully over a fallen log and sticking the landing.

Reaching the opposite end of the woods, Eli kicked on his Zip-Slippers. He skated down the Arcadia dry canal and wheeled to a suave stop in front of a concrete wall.

"What's the big idea, pencil neck?" asked

NotEnrique, hearing Strickler, Nomura, and Steve's voices getting closer.

"We're going to Trollmarket—*duh*!" said Eli, producing the Horngazel from his pocket.

"How, uh, how do ya know about that?" NotEnrique said, now getting nervous.

"Jim said that Gunmar fella took over Trollmarket," explained Eli while studying the wall. "And this canal is where I saw those two Trolls heading when they ran past my bedroom months ago, with their stone for skin. Ergo, the entrance has gotta be around here somewhere. And like you said, lil' guy—this Horngazel is the key."

"Who're you callin' little, ya—?" NotEnrique groused before Eli thrust the Horngazel—handle first—into his open mouth like a baby pacifier.

"But I figure it can only be used by a Troll," added Eli.

Steve, Strickler, and Nomura reached the canal in time to see Eli drag NotEnrique's face in a straight line across the wall. Eli's glasses reflected with blue light as the line glowed. He quickly sketched two more lines with the Horngazel protruding from NotEnrique's lips, creating the rectangular outline of a human door. He paused to admire his work.

"Eli!" shouted Steve.

"I told you—call me Romeo!" Eli said.

The Horngazel doorway crumbled inward, and NotEnrique spat out the crystal key like a petulant baby. Over the grinding of the stones floating around the otherworldly tunnel, Nomura warned, "Don't go in there, kid! You have no idea of the monster waiting on the other side!"

"'These violent delights have violent ends'!" Eli quoted again before blowing a kiss and diving headfirst into the swirling corridor with NotEnrique.

Hurrying down the angled canal wall, Strickler, Nomura, and Steve jumped into the tunnel after them. Remembering something, Steve stepped back out and retrieved the crystal key.

"Gross!" said Steve, wiping NotEnrique's drool onto his pant leg.

Strickler and Nomura's arms reached out of the Horngazel tunnel and yanked Steve back inside before it closed completely.

"Whoa!" gasped Eli as took in the full scope of Heartstone Trollmarket. "What a dump."

Ever since he had first heard of a secret society of Trolls living beneath his feet, Eli had dreamed they lived in some vast and vibrant subterranean metropolis. Instead, he found a drab military state teeming with regiments of Gumm-Gumm soldiers.

"Aw, no," muttered NotEnrique, pulling free of Eli. "Look what they did to this place. . . ."

The elfin Changeling looked up at the Heartstone, which once shone with warm, amber light. Now, however, black veins of rot shot through the crystal, darkening Trollmarket. NotEnrique only looked away when he spotted Eli strolling over to the Hero's Forge without a care in the world. Strickler, Nomura, and an extremely tense Steve caught up with NotEnrique, watching from an elevated bluff as Eli slipped undetected into the arena.

"He's going to get himself killed," said Nomura.

"Worse," Strickler replied. "He's going to get *all* of us killed."

Eli walked into the training pit at the center of the Hero's Forge. Long shadows blackened its carved fixtures. He whistled and said, "Man, outta all the places I've seen as a Creepslayer, this one's the creepiest, that's for sure."

Looking up, Eli saw three Trolls staring back at him in dumbfounded amazement from a throne at the top of the arena. One was a blind six-eyed Troll. One was a tall Krubera, her regal face lit up by bioluminescent patterns. And the last was the biggest Gumm-Gumm Eli had ever seen, his veins flecked with gold, his one remaining eye burning with fury.

"Oh, hey, there," said Eli with a friendly wave. "Is one of you Gunmar?"

"How dare you address our Dark Underlord?" demanded Dictatious. "I'd throttle you myself . . . if I could see you."

"Another human, here in Trollmarket?" said Queen Usurna in an insulted voice.

The Gumm-Gumm king silenced Dictatious and Usurna and announced, "I am he who you foolishly seek. I am Gunmar the Gold. Tell me your name, whelp, before I grind your organs into paste."

"I am Romeo," said Eli, standing akimbo. "And the only thing turning to paste around here is you, *Dumb*-mar!"

Back on the bluff, Steve chuckled and said, "Heh. Good one."

"Unbelievable," Nomura gasped. "Is it possible

Gunmar's even bigger—even stronger—here than he was in the Darklands?"

"He's feeding off the Heartstone," said Strickler. "And poisoning it in the process, by the looks of things. I . . . I never fully realized what horrors we've helped bring into this world."

In the Hero's Forge, Gunmar's eye narrowed at the interloper before him. "You certainly have gronk-nuks, fleshbag. I'll give you that."

Eli stopped mooning Gunmar long enough to say, "That's not all I've got, sucka! Back on the surface, there's an entire army of Trolls itching for a fight!"

"The little twit's gonna give away our location!" cried NotEnrique on the bluff. "We gotta shut him up now!"

Gunmar pounded his golden fist against his throne, breaking off a piece of it, and roared, "Where? Tell me where the Trollhunter and his rabble hide from my vengeance!"

"You want to know where?" said Eli.

Desperate to silence Eli, Strickler transformed into his Changeling self, causing Steve to promptly faint at his scaly green feet. Reaching under his cloak, Strickler flicked a feather dart toward the Hero's Forge.

"I'll tell you where!" Eli yelled up at Gunmar.

The feather dart soared across Trollmarket and whizzed right past Eli's throat—severing the Grit-Shaka necklace. The totem fell to the arena floor, and Eli held a hand to his head, feeling woozy all of a sudden.

"Where . . . where . . . ," stammered Eli. "Where am I?"

He adjusted his glasses and saw Gunmar the Gold, as if for the first time. Eli whimpered pitifully and squeaked out a simple "Uh-oh."

CHAPTER 14
MERLIN'S MISTAKE

Jim worried about Gogun, even as his friends and Blinky's Troll followers made their way toward Glastonbury Tor Trollmarket's vault. He peeked around corners and poked his head into abandoned caves, but still found no sign of the crotchety old hermit.

Probably doing the Troll tango under another bridge somewhere, Jim thought.

"At last," said Blinky, reaching the vault's fortified doors. "Now, does anyone here happen to know the combination?"

The two young brothers pushed their way to the front of the crowd. Blinky gave them a wide berth, avoiding eye contact with the siblings. The eldest put two of his four green hands on a pair of tumblers. He rotated them a few degrees in one direction, then back a few in the other. With a groan of heavy gears, three overlapping doors sank in in rapid succession, revealing the open vault beyond them.

"Why thank you, Dic—er, young lad," Blinky said carefully.

"Of course, Gronka Morka," replied young Dictatious, taking his little brother by the hands. "Perhaps you'll repay the favor one day."

Blinky saw his younger self and brother return to the crowd and said, "Yes . . . perhaps."

Inside the vault, Toby and AAARRRGGHH!!! dug through the many relics lining its thick crystal walls. In his haste, Toby accidentally bumped his backside against a pile of delicate Troll items, spilling them to the floor—and revealing a Kairosect underneath.

"Bingo," grumbled AAARRRGGHH!!!

"Tobes, you found it!" Jim said, taking the Kairosect from his best friend.

"Yeah—and this bad boy too!" Toby replied as he then pulled his Warhammer from another mound of Troll gear.

Claire sniffled and added, "Great work, Toby!

Now all we need to get home is—"

"This?" said a sinister voice behind them, followed by the peep of an adorable *meow*.

Team Trollhunters' joy faded. They all turned around and saw Tellad-Urr the Terrible gently cradling Shmorkrarg in one red claw and holding Gogun by the throat in the other. The dark Trollhunter nodded to the Shadow Staff hitched to his hip. Behind him, the freed prisoners scattered to all corners of their market in fear.

"You turn up nearly as often as this accursed Amulet," Tellad-Urr said to Jim.

"Let Gogun go," Jim said back. "And Shmorkie."

"Yeah," gurgled Gogun. "This seems like it's between the two of you and not really any of my business—urk!"

Tellad-Urr tightened his grip around Gogun, but eased the kitten to the ground. He then considered the old Troll in his clutches and said, "You would risk your life to save this coward?"

"He's going to become a Trollhunter," Jim answered defiantly. "Just like me. Just like you used to be, Tellad-Urr."

"Not for much longer," muttered the dark

Trollhunter ominously as he glared at Jim.

Before Team Trollhunters had a chance to react, four more Tellad-Urr replicas zoomed around them. With lightning-fast speed, the duplicates struck down Jim, Toby, Claire, Blinky, and AAARRRGGHH!!! in a flurry of scarlet fists.

And now he's got Araknak the Agile's quickness, Jim thought just before his body hit the ground.

"You come from the future, yet you do not perceive the inherent flaw in all Trollhunters," said the original Tellad-Urr, tossing aside Gogun like so much garbage.

The River Troll's smock snagged the Shadow Staff on his way down, dislodging it from Tellad-Urr's hip and sending it clattering across the vault floor. The dark Trollhunter did not seem to care, he was so consumed with his tirade, saying, "We must be strong enough to protect those around us, even as the Amulet erodes at our resolve, century after agonizing century. This is the wizard's folly. This is Merlin's mistake."

"The only mistake I see is your own," said Jim, struggling to push himself off the ground.

"Do you really think you will spend the rest of your life as a Trollhunter?" asked Tellad-Urr. "Do you truly picture yourself carrying this mantle day after day? Barely able to swing your sword in old age? Pushing away those you love? Giving up pieces of yourself along the way?"

"I . . . I don't know," Jim answered truthfully, an image of his mom alone in their kitchen popping into his mind. "But do *you* really think Gunmar and Bular will honor your deal? They're gonna double-cross you the second they overthrow Orlagk. Trust me, I've read about it!"

Tellad-Urr the Terrible's devastated face twisted into contemptuous look—even as his four duplicates glanced at each other in concern.

"Do . . . do you think it's possible?" asked the second Tellad-Urr.

"Treachery is always possible with Gumm-Gumms," said the third.

"That seems to be all there is these days," mused the fourth ruefully. "Treachery."

"If only we—I—could go back and do things differently," the fifth now said. "Broken bones and endless obligation might not seem so painful if traveling the virtuous path once more."

"NO!" roared the first Tellad-Urr, absorbing the quarrelsome quartet into his Amulet. "No more argument! No more voices or ticking or sacrifice!"

The dark Trollhunter stormed over to Gogun's battered body, raising the hackles of the startled kittens gathered around him. Tellad-Urr pressed one red boot on top of the old Troll's chest and pledged, "I will never pass Merlin's misery on to another. History *will* change."

"You can change, too," said Jim, now on his feet. "Anyone can."

"You lie!" Tellad-Urr snapped.

"No lie," AAARRRGGHH!!! said as he rose next to Jim. "I change."

"Aarghaumont speaks true, Tellad-Urr," Blinky interjected as he Toby, and Claire recovered. "He once fought on the side of the Gumm-Gumms as one of their strongest warriors. Yet his true strength lay inside, making his miraculous change of heart possible."

"You can be triumphant again," Claire said, quickly tucking her hand under her coat.

Gogun cracked open one fearful eye as Tellad-Urr

lifted his boot. The dark Trollhunter's lopsided face seemed to soften as he considered these five strangers' words. Turning his back on them, Tellad-Urr braced his hands on one of the thick walls, as if steadying himself. Jim and his friends looked hopefully to each other—until Tellad-Urr dug his claws into the wall. The dark Trollhunter excavated an enormous hunk of crystal from the vault, raised it over his one-horned head, and uttered, "Not if I can help it."

Jim, Claire, Toby, Blinky, and AAARRRGGHH!!! had just enough time to share one last, desperate look before Tellad-Urr the Terrible slammed the crystal wall down upon them.

CHAPTER 15
MESS WITH THE TROLL, GET THE HORNS

"DIE!" commanded Gunmar the Gold, his primal roar echoing across the Hero's Forge. "I will see this *Row-Muh-Oh* die!"

Eli screamed out of the arena and into the dark Trollmarket. All around him, hundreds of Gunmar's Gumm-Gumms poured from every cave and tunnel. The helmeted soldiers converged, pointing their Parlok Spears at Eli's trembling body—until a series of explosions rocked the underground city. The detonations sent Gumm-Gumms flying this way and that, clearing a path for Eli.

"Run, Romeo, run!" yelled Steve, now awake and lobbing more Dwärkstone grenades.

"Who?!" said Eli as he scrambled to safety.

"I thought we confiscated all those," said

Strickler, reverting to his human form.

"Oh yeah, like I'm gonna listen to what one of my teachers says!" Steve replied sarcastically. "Especially one who turns into a creep!"

Steve took off down the bluff, and the Changelings followed. Eli met them at the base of a spiral staircase, its crystal steps dim like the Heartstone, and hugged his fellow Creepslayer.

"You saved my life, Steve!" Eli said, catching his breath. "How can I ever repay you?"

"By never hugging me again," Steve answered with a hard shove. "But I, uh . . . I'm glad you're alive, Pepperbuddy."

"That ain't gonna last for long," said NotEnrique, looking back at the wave of recovered Gumm-Gumms racing toward them. "I could really go for a glug right now."

Unfazed, Strickler pointed up the crystal staircase and said, "The Horngazel access point is that way. Let's move quickly, before—"

A blue, spiked ball suddenly rolled in front of the steps, blocking them. It then unfurled, revealing a muscular Troll with a metal arm, nose ring, and mirrored eyes. To Nomura it looked like—

"Draal?" Nomura gasped at the Troll. "What's happened to you?"

Draal stepped toward them, malice shining in his chromed gaze. The Changelings and Creepslayerz backed away as the spiked Troll wordlessly advanced, while the phalanx of Gumm-Gumm soldiers closed in from the rear.

"I'm afraid he's not Draal anymore, Nomura," Strickler said. "At least, not the one you knew. Gunmar's Decimaar Blade has seen to that."

Nomura's face fell in sorrow before Draal tucked back into a ball again and spiraled toward them. Steeling herself, Nomura grabbed Steve and Eli by their collars and jumped out of the way. Strickler and NotEnrique leaped aside with their incredible Changeling reflexes. Draal barreled right past his targets and slammed into the oncoming Gumm-Gumms, scattering them like tenpins. Unfortunately, Queen Usurna and her Krubera Trolls now descended upon the scene, barring the path to the crystal staircase once more.

"You heard your Dark Underlord," Usurna cried to her Kruberas. "Kill the intruders!"

"Oh no, what have I done?" Eli moaned.

"I've doomed my best friend and three innocent shape-shifters!"

"We're far from innocent," Nomura clarified.

"And what's this 'best friend' business?" asked Steve.

"We're not doomed just yet," Strickler said. "There may be one last way out!"

Strickler broke off to the side, and the others ran after him—as did Draal, the Gumm-Gumms, and the Kruberas. The five fleeing figures seemed so tiny compared to the onslaught of deranged Trolls that threatened to engulf them. Running deeper below Dark Trollmarket, the Changelings and Creepslayerz rushed onto a platform that contained a spherical Troll vehicle.

"The gyre!" NotEnrique said as he hopped inside of the conveyance. "You two fleshbags may wanna buckle up!"

Steve and Eli entered the gyre and did as instructed, while the collective howl of enemy Trolls rumbled closer. Nomura saw the gyre tunnel blocked by a gigantic hangar door and said, "We're trapped."

"Not necessarily," Strickler said as he stood at

the vehicle's controls, ignoring the nearing Trolls. "Not unless Misters Palchuk and Pepperjack are finally out of their 'smoke bombs'?"

Steve and Eli turned their backs to the others. Nomura thought she heard the sound of zippers. When the Creepslayerz turned around again, they held two last Dwärkstones.

"Disgusting," NotEnrique said with a shudder.

"Says the green guy wearing a *diaper*," Steve quipped as he and Eli threw the grenades.

The door blasted to smithereens, revealing an infinite network of underground tunnels. As Draal, the Gumm-Gumms, and the Kruberas stampeded toward the platform, Strickler cranked a control lever and yelled, "Hang on!"

The gyre launched down the tunnels like a rocketing armillary, transporting two Creepslayerz and three Changelings away from their pursuers and out of Dark Trollmarket.

"They . . . they escaped, Dark Underlord," admitted Queen Usurna as she led Dictatious toward the Heartstone, their heads bowed in shame.

Gunmar didn't even bother looking at his cowed

advisors. He merely pressed his claws against the colossal crystal, leeching more of its life-giving energies. New black tendrils of decay snaked through the Heartstone, even as Gunmar's veins pulsated with a golden sheen.

"You tell me what I already know," said Gunmar the Gold. "Or have you forgotten that Draal's possessed sight is now my own?"

Dictatious cleared his throat and said, "Sire, if I might suggest—"

"Stay your tongue, lest I render it as useless as those six cataracts you call eyes," Gunmar interrupted. "I've suffered your lacking advisements— and these humans' interference—for far too long. But no more."

The Gumm-Gumm king's eye flared with malevolence as he said, "Send my best trackers above to this *Arr-Cay-Dee-Uh*. Tell them to hunt the Trollhunter and only return with his remains—and those of all he holds dear—clenched between their grisly jaws!"

CHAPTER 16
CLASH OF THE GUMM-GUMMS

Is this Heaven? wondered Jim when he woke up surrounded by clouds.

But the thought quickly vanished when he rolled over and found his best friend lying beside him, noisily chewing. Toby smiled sheepishly, offered Jim another candy bar, and said, "Nougat Nummie?"

"Maybe later," answered Jim.

He stood up in the moors, a thick blanket of predawn fog still swirling around his feet. Jim then saw Blinky and AAARRRGGHH!!!'s heads poke out of the mist. The Trolls appeared just as confused. Jim cupped his hands around his mouth and yelled, "Claire!"

"Up here," called Claire's voice from above.

The rest of Team Trollhunters turned their gaze

skyward as Claire descended from a closing shadow portal, the Shadow Staff held firmly in her hand.

"How'd you get it back?" asked Toby. "And how come we're not, y'know, *smooshed*?"

"I snagged my Shadow Staff off the vault floor while Tellad-Urr was busy arguing with himself," explained Claire as she alighted. "That's how I was able to jump us out of there right before he flattened us . . . and this."

She pulled her other arm from behind her back, revealing the intact Kairosect.

"Nice going, Nuñez," said Jim, tucking the silver streak behind her ear. "You're as sneaky as you are beautiful."

"Schweet!" cheered Toby. "Now we have everything we need to head back home! Let's all click our heels together three times and say, 'There's no place like Nana's!'"

A low, steady beat echoed across the moors. Blinky narrowed his six eyes to peer through the haze and said, "Those are Gumm-Gumm war drums."

Team Trollhunters watched in dread as two opposing armies convened in the foggy valley below

Glastonbury Tor. Orlagk the Oppressor led one side forward, while Gunmar and Bular stood at the vanguard of the other. Both camps came prepared for battle, yet Gunmar's seemed the better-armed force with their weapons of burnished metal.

"Clash of the Gumm-Gumms," AAARRRGGHH!!! said balefully.

"Not that we don't appreciate your saving us in the proverbial nick of time, Claire," said Blinky. "But did you have to drop us right into the middle of Gunmar's historic rebellion?"

"And look who has ringside seats," Jim said.

He spotted Gogun at the edge of the battlefield, now fettered in the same types of chains that once held Toby, Blinky, and AAARRRGGHH!!! Tellad-Urr the Terrible stood beside the old River Troll, watching the two Gumm-Gumm armies collide in all-out war. The Gumm-Gumms' battle cries reverberated around the moors. Jim and the others could hear Bular's elaborate death threats and the orders barking from Orlagk's mismatched jaws.

"Well, I guess that's our cue to leave," Toby shrugged matter-of-factly.

"I . . . I can't," said Jim, surprising his friends.

"Believe me, nobody wants to get home more than me. But I can't just leave Gogun out there like that. If Tellad-Urr doesn't kill him, one of those Gumm-Gumms will."

"Master Jim," began Blinky, clapping his four hands along Jim's arms. "I know you—"

"Please, Blinky," Jim interceded. "No offense, but if this is another lecture about not altering the natural flow of the space-time whatever, I already know the drill."

Blinky smiled at his champion and said, "On the contrary, Trollhunter. I merely wished to repeat what a wise young man once told me: 'History is written by the victors.'"

Jim smiled back, galvanized by Blinky's words, and said, "Then let's go be victorious!"

Gogun cringed as another Gumm-Gumm collapsed before him. Tellad-Urr kicked the battered body aside, then yanked on Gogun's shackles to make him keep up. The dark Trollhunter waded through the battle on a direct path to Orlagk, dragging Gogun behind him.

"Oh, why didn't I stay under that bridge?" Gogun

whined to the kittens under his smock.

"Your regrets will soon come to an end," said Tellad-Urr. "Both of ours will."

Seeing an opportunity to strike, Tellad-Urr released Gogun's chains and ran toward Orlagk. The Oppressor raised his Decimaar Blade just in time to repel his crimson enemy's Sundown Mace.

"Attacked from within and without, am I?" Orlagk snarled through his overbite. "No matter! This simply makes it easier for me to slay all my nemeses at once!"

Their weapons met again with a ringing clang. The noise startled Gogun's kittens, making his favorite scamper into the midst of the battlefield. Held in place by his heavy chains, the old Troll could only reach out and cry, "Shmorkrarg!"

"Funny, I once knew a cat named Shmorkrarg," said Jim as he scooped up the helpless kitten and returned her to her rightful owner. "Although I hear that's a pretty common name."

"Kim!" said Gogun. "I am as happy to see you as I am furious we met in the first place."

"I'll take that as a 'thank you,'" joked Jim.

He set about picking the Gogun's shackles with

more of Toby's dental wire, unaware of the Gumm-Gumm soldier sneaking up behind him. Before Gogun could warn him, Toby's Warhammer smacked the Gumm-Gumm back into the fog of war.

"Thanks, Tobes!" Jim said, still fiddling with the locks.

"What're time-traveling friends for?" Toby asked, then hurtled his Warhammer.

The enchanted mallet flew across the battlefield and connected with the face of another Gumm-Gumm that had been choking Blinky. The six-eyed Troll gave Toby four grateful thumbs up, then tossed the unconscious soldier into one of the many shadow portals summoned by Claire. She projected her next black hole in front of AAARRRGGHH!!!, who galloped into it. An instant later, he emerged out of the matching portal behind enemy lines. AAARRRGGHH!!! swatted away warring Gumm-Gumms in droves, knocking them right out of their helmets. He then cocked his fist and struck at another soldier—only to pull his punch at the last second.

AAARRRGGHH!!!'s runes faded as he stared the young Krubera in front of him. It was like looking into a mirror. The young Troll's horns were stubbier and his shoulders were barely covered in mossy green fur, yet AAARRRGGHH!!! recognized the face, for it was his own.

"You look . . . like me," said teen AAARRRGGHH!!! before he decked his grown-up self.

The two AAARRRGGHH!!!s grappled across the moors, tumbling right past Tellad-Urr and Orlagk. The dark Trollhunter swung his Sundown Mace at the snaggle-toothed Gumm-Gumm and said, "You should've killed me while you had the chance, Oppressor!"

"You were too pathetic to be put out of your misery, Trollhunter!" snarled Orlagk.

The mace clipped him on its return swing, and Orlagk felt his Decimaar Blade fade. He looked up, uneven jaws agape, as his crimson combatant loomed over him. Tellad-Urr the Terrible relished the moment. He raised the Sundown Mace over his one horn, ready to deliver a final, crushing blow to Orlagk, when a peculiar sight arrested the dark Trollhunter's attention.

Past the fog, through the acrid smoke of war, he saw that human boy—the one with the look-alike Amulet, the one who had somehow cheated death yet again—freeing the old Troll. Forgetting Orlagk for the moment, Tellad-Urr stomped past the Gumm-Gumms that attacked each other around him and yelled, "You!"

Jim pulled the last chain off Gogun just before the dark Trollhunter lifted him bodily off the field of battle. His ruined face quivering in fury, Tellad-Urr pulled Jim close and asked, "Why? Why do you persist in doing the wizard's bidding? Why endanger yourself time and again for those too weak to defend themselves?"

"It's the right thing to do," said Jim. "I . . . I never needed an Amulet to tell me that."

Tellad-Urr the Terrible stared at Jim, his emotions clearly in conflict beneath that weary, abused face. He tightened his hold around Jim's neck and mentally bid the claws on his free hand to grow even sharper. Bracing for the worst, Jim shut his eyes and lamented that one last dinner with his mom that he would never have.

With a scream of unbridled anguish, Tellad-Urr dug his claw not into Jim's face—but into the Amulet embedded in his scarlet breastplate. He dug the ticking device free of his body, making the barbed Sundown Armor turn as immaterial as the fog about them. Tellad-Urr then released Jim, opened the Amulet, and removed the red gem given to him by Gunmar.

Falling beside Gogun, Jim looked up at the one-horned Troll. Now laid bare in the absence of his armor, Tellad-Urr's body showed the numerous lacing scars it had acquired in its years of service. Jim's eyes watered in empathy. Clearly, this was a Trollhunter who had suffered in his tour of duty. With a deep, shuddering breath, Tellad-Urr dropped the gemstone onto the battlefield and ground it to red, sparkling dust under his heel.

"Merlin, forgive me . . . ," whispered the formerly dark Trollhunter.

No sooner had the prayer left his lips than two matching swords sank into his back. Jim and Gogun watched a look of long-awaited relief spread across Tellad-Urr's face before his body hit the ground—and revealed Bular behind it.

CHAPTER 17
IT'S BEEN EDUCATIONAL

The gyre erupted out of the earth. It ricocheted between the trees in Arcadia's woods like a pinball before finally coming to rest at the end of a long furrow. Strickler, Nomura, NotEnrique, Steve, and Eli each staggered out of the vehicle—dizzy, but very much alive.

"That . . . that was . . . ," Eli stammered.

"The worst field trip I've ever been on! I'd rather go back to that boring museum," finished Steve.

NotEnrique thought about it, then said, "Eh. I've been on more unpleasant gyre rides than that."

"I suppose I do have some experience driving away from bloodthirsty Trolls," Strickler mused, then looked up at the moon over the sky. "There's still a few hours before sunrise. We need to find

Kilfred and the other Trolls. That is, *if* they weren't already discovered during our impromptu jaunt to Trollmarket."

The Creepslayerz and Changelings heard a ringing sound carry through the woods.

"That's the school bell!" Eli exclaimed.

"At four in the morning?" Nomura asked suspiciously.

Kilfred studied his own reflection in the glossy surface of a soccer trophy before he tossed the award into his mouth and swallowed it whole.

"Hey! That was mine!" hissed Steve as Eli and the Changelings pulled him back into Strickler's old office. "I won it fair and square against those punks at Arcadia Oaks Academy!"

The group peeked their heads back out of Strickler's door. The Troll mob rifled through the rest of the high school's trophy case, as well as many of the student lockers. They ate old gym socks, wiped their noses on textbooks, and turned the teachers' lounge into their own personal toilet. And in the principal's office, Bagdwella accidentally pressed the public-address button again, setting off the school bell one more time.

"It was nice of Mr. Strickler to let us into school through his secret passage," whispered Eli. "But how do we get the Trolls *out*?"

Before anybody could answer, Kilfred's four followers appeared in front of Strickler's door, fogging the window glass with their breath.

"Hide!" Nomura ordered, but it was too late.

The Trolls barged into the office, grabbing her, NotEnrique, and Strickler—but failing to notice the Creepslayerz, who now hid in the secret passage behind Strickler's bookcase. Steve and Eli heard the Changelings scuffle with the Trolls for a moment, then everything went silent. Cracking open the bookcase a hair, the boys found the office empty and disordered from the recent struggle. Even the masks that adorned Strickler's space had been knocked to the floor.

"Um, they'd understand if we just went home now, right?" asked Steve.

"I dunno," Eli answered, picking one of the masks from the floor. "I guess I would've understood if you all left 'Romeo' in Trollmarket. But you didn't."

Steve nodded in solemn understanding and

whispered, "Goblins and ghoulies and things that go 'boo.' We will pound into goo. We are coming for you."

"Friendship forever will stop all the creepers," Eli continued with the next verse. "We know all the secrets, for we are the keepers . . ."

". . . of awesome," Steve finished.

As the Creepslayerz started their elaborate handshake, Kilfred's four Troll students hauled Strickler, Nomura, and NotEnrique into the school gymnasium. They tossed the Changelings onto the blue padded mats, prompting NotEnrique to gripe, "Oi! Easy on the goods, old timers!"

"Ah, a trio of Impures in our midst," said Kilfred from atop the highest bleacher, wearing deflated dodgeballs on his horns like ornamental jewelry. "Bind them with the sacred trusses!"

Nomura rolled her eyes as the Trolls tied her, Strickler, and NotEnrique with jump ropes.

"I really don't think Coach Lawrence will appreciate your misuse of athletic equipment, Kilfred," said Strickler. "Perhaps we could discuss this . . . back at the warehouse?"

"Never!" bellowed Kilfred, his black-and-white fur rippling. "This *Hig-Uh Such-Ool* shall be our

Troll kingdom once we gain control of the surface world from the fleshbags!"

"That's 'high school,' skunk-beard!" NotEnrique corrected.

"And the only one who shall rule the surface world . . . is I," said a guttural voice.

The Trolls and Changelings all turned, and the color drained from each and every one of their faces. Gunmar the Gold stood before the gym's swinging doors, his one eye incensed.

"Great Gorgus, it's Gunmar!" cried Kilfred.

"But . . . how?" asked Strickler.

"I followed you through your gyre tunnel," Gunmar said. "And now I shall devour you and— and do other things after that. Evil things!"

"Noooo!" yelled Steve as he ran out of the boys' locker room, swinging a folding chair. "You may have eaten poor Eli, but you'll never eat me!"

"Ow!" roared Gunmar as Steve hit him with the folding chair. "You shall pay for that, human I have never met before. And the price—is your life!"

Gunmar wrapped his golden claw around Steve's head and began to squeeze, causing Steve to scream, "Aaaaah! This is worse than algebra!"

The horrific sight made Kilfred and the other Trolls run screaming out of the gym's other exit. But Nomura, still tied up, saw the sky brighten through the windows and said, "It's nearly morning! You'll all turn to stone out there!"

The panicked Trolls hesitated, trapped between Gunmar the Gold and the rising sun.

"Use the tunnel in my office!" said Strickler. "It'll lead you underground to the woods. From there, you can find the warehouse. Hurry!"

Kilfred's mob raced out of the gymnasium and down the hallway toward Strickler's office. Now alone with the Changelings, Gunmar dropped Steve's twitching body, roller-skated to the mats, and pulled off his own face—revealing Eli with a Tiki-like mask in his hands.

"That was quite the performance, Misters Palchuk and Pepperjack," Strickler said with admiration. "I see you found the Glamour Mask hidden among the other decorations in my office."

"It looked like the one we took from that crate earlier," admitted Eli. "I heard you say nothing short of Gunmar would scare the Trolls back to the warehouse, so I put two and two together and—"

"Geez, Eli, nobody wants to hear your life story!" said Steve.

"Sorry," Eli mumbled, then turned to face Ms. Nomura. "And I'm sorry for kissing you without your permission. I guess I wasn't acting like myself."

Nomura arched her eyebrow and said, "'Thus from my lips, by thine, my sin is purged.'"

"'Then have my lips the sin that they have took,'" sighed Eli, completing the quote.

"This is incredibly awkward," said NotEnrique before they started hearing police sirens. "Cheese it, it's the fuzz!"

The Changelings and Creepslayerz took in the vandalized high school around them. The empty mole mascot costume fell from the rafters, where it had been thrown earlier by Kilfred. Strickler shook his head in dismay and said, "Somehow, I doubt Detective Scott will buy a second phony eyewitness account from me."

"You guys beat it," said Steve to the Changelings. "The Creepslayerz'll handle this one."

"We will?" asked Eli.

"You know it, Pepperbuddy." Steve grinned, a plan forming in his mind. . . .

CHAPTER 18
THE WHITE KNIGHT

Tellad-Urr's Amulet slipped out of his hand as Bular removed his twin blades. The device rolled across the battlefield and settled right in front of Jim and Gogun, who now hid behind a pile of fallen Gumm-Gumms.

"Take it!" Jim whispered, pointing to the Amulet.

"No!" Gogun whispered back.

"Yes!" Jim insisted.

Gogun pouted, reluctantly picked up the Amulet, and . . . nothing happened.

"I . . . I don't get it . . . ," Jim said, gobsmacked.

But his eyes widened as strands of arcane energy wisped out of Gogun's Amulet and into his own. The old Troll dropped his device like it was suddenly hot. As it once again siphoned power from its counterpart, Jim's Amulet glowed brighter than it ever had before, the blue magic now verging on white. Bular lurked nearby, and the incandescent display caught his attention.

"You better run and save yourself, Gogun," said Jim before he turned and saw that the old Troll was already long gone, running for the hills.

"Thanks!" called the fleeing Gogun without breaking his stride.

"Maybe we found the wrong Gogun after all," Jim muttered before raising his supercharged Amulet. "For the glory of Merlin, Daylight is mine to command!"

Bular shielded his eyes from the supernova. When the rapturous waves of light and heat faded, the son of Gunmar lowered his arms and encountered something he had never before seen.

Jim stood transformed before Bular. His armor, normally silver, now shone a blinding white, as if composed of solid light. The Shield and Sword of Starlight manifested in Jim's hand, and his horned helmet concealed his true, human identity beneath its lambent faceplate.

"What manner of being are you?" barked Bular incredulously.

"I'm the Trollhunter," answered Jim. "And one day, I'll be the last thing you ever see."

"Big talk from such a small Troll," said Bular, drawing his blades from their crossed scabbards. "I may fall in battle one day—but not *this* day!"

Bular lunged at the white knight, only to be slammed off-course by a far larger Gumm-Gumm. Both Jim and Bular looked up and saw Orlagk the Oppressor between them, reforming the Decimaar Blade in his claw. Drool dripped from his tangled teeth as he said, "We shall see about that, traitor. Your mutinous father's too busy fighting off my legions to come to your aid."

Orlagk then pointed his jagged weapon at Jim, adding, "And you will join Tellad-Urr in the unmarked grave of forgotten fools!"

With that Orlagk slashed his Decimaar Blade at Jim—who deflected with his Shield of Starlight—and then struck at Bular in the same fluid motion. Bular blocked with one of his swords while stabbing at the Trollhunter with its mate.

"Holy sheesh-kabobs!" said Jim, finding himself stuck in a three-way fight to the death. "If anyone else from the future can hear me, I could sure use some backup right about now!"

AAARRRGGHH!!! would've been all too happy to help—if his teenaged self wasn't busy punching him in the skull. Rolling away from the next falling fist, AAARRRGGHH!!! grabbed one of the Gumm-Gumm helmets abandoned on the battlefield and fit it over his head.

"Why you look like me?" demanded the teen-aged Krubera.

"Umm . . . no I don't," said AAARRRGGHH!!!, his voice muffled under the helmet.

Teen AAARRRGGHH!!! rammed into adult AAARRRGGHH!!!, and they traded blows again. The war raging around them paled in comparison to their slobber-knocker of a fight. Their identical runes glowing with identical fury, the two Krubera tussled in an even match—until the grown-up AAARRRGGHH!!! trapped his teen self in a bear hug.

"Calm down," AAARRRGGHH!!! said through his helmet.

"Gumm-Gumms never surrender!" the struggling teen AAARRRGGHH!!! grunted.

"You not Gumm-Gumm," AAARRRGGHH!!! said. "Not if you not want to be."

The gentle giant squeezed harder and felt his younger self finally go lax. The older Krubera eased his teenaged body onto the moors and said, "You cross that bridge . . . one day."

AAARRRGGHH!!! then removed the helmet, crushed it underfoot, and reentered the fray. He charged toward Blinky, Toby, and Claire, who still fought in the midst of the civil war. And beyond them, one illuminating figure fended off the dual attacks of two Gumm-Gumms.

"I think I liked it better . . . when you were fighting . . . each other!" panted Jim, dodging Orlagk and swiping at Bular.

"Who said we stopped?" asked Orlagk.

The Oppressor clobbered Bular with the butt of his Decimaar Blade, and Jim watched the dazed brute collapse onto his knees. A troop of Orlagk's soldiers arrived, placed a sack over Bular's head, and dragged him away by his arms.

"Save that one for ransom," ordered Orlagk. "We'll use him to force Gunmar's surrender, then hang father and son with the same noose."

Jim didn't know why he hadn't thought about it before—perhaps it was because he hadn't slept a wink since arriving in this era—but hearing Orlagk say Gunmar's name reminded the Trollhunter of his time in the Darklands. Of someone he met there, who saved his life even as she sacrificed her own for the sake of revenge. Jim remained mindful of Blinky's warnings about altering the course of history. And yet, when presented with the chance to save one life, if not *thousands* of lives, how could he do nothing?

"Orlagk, there's something you need to know about Gunmar," Jim started to say. "Something that affects you and your d—"

Orlagk suddenly hammered the shimmering Trollhunter with his horns, knocking the wind out of him. Jim fell to the trampled field of heather. He struggled to remain conscious, watching his luminous Starlight Armor evaporate and the borrowed energy leave his Amulet.

"A human Trollhunter?" Orlagk cackled at Jim's exposed form. "That, I did not foresee."

"Or this," said an old voice before a gleaming fist came out of nowhere and broke Orlagk's already deformed jaw.

Jim's vision cleared just in time to see Orlagk

drop. He then looked to the champion who defeated the Oppressor with a single punch—although Jim had to rub his eyes to make sure he wasn't hallucinating from a concussion.

"No way . . . ," said Jim, his disbelieving eyes almost as wide as his smile.

Gogun smiled back awkwardly, his frail body now clad in the Daylight Armor of the Trollhunter. Tapping the Amulet he inherited from Tellad-Urr, Gogun said, "I suppose I needed to *earn* this before I could get it to work. Sorry I ran away."

"Which time?" asked Jim as Gogun helped him to his feet. "Just kidding. That's all river water under the footbridge now."

AAARRRGGHH!!!, Blinky, Toby, and Claire rushed up at once, pleasantly surprised to see Gogun wearing the silver vestments of the Trollhunter.

"Great Gron—" Blinky began before catching himself. "That is to say—oh me, oh my."

Orlagk stirred awake. He reformed his Decimaar Blade and took a step toward Gogun.

"You want to dance?" the Trollhunter asked, standing his ground just as Jim and his time-tossed friends stood beside him. "Let's dance."

Easily outnumbered and clearly humiliated, Orlagk the Oppressor turned tail and ran away. The scattered remnants of both Gumm-Gumm armies soon followed suit, retreating into the dark corners of the moors.

As day broke above them, Claire cast a shadow over their group, protecting Blinky, AAARRRGGHH!!!, and Gogun from the sunlight. They stood in silence over Tellad-Urr's still body, paying their respects to a hero who had fallen in more ways than one. And although he could no longer see it, the one-horned, one-time Trollhunter finally found peace under the red skies of his first—and last—sunrise.

"I believe everything's in order," said Blinky, examining the Kairosect in his four hands. "If only there was a way to replicate the distressed condition of the *other* Kairosect."

Toby took the time-altering device from Blinky and intentionally dropped it on the ground. The Kairosect cracked open, its innards now sparking with arcs of green electricity.

"That works," grumbled AAARRRGGHH!!! behind them. "Nice one, Wingman."

"It's a gift," Toby said with a humble shrug.

The three of them one last look at Glastonbury Tor Trollmarket around them. The purple Heartstone pulsed brighter than before from the cavern ceiling, and the many freed Trolls gave Blinky appreciative waves as they returned to their homes. A few feet away, the newly-minted Trollhunter shook Claire's hand and then Jim's.

"Take care of yourself, Gogun," said Claire.

"You do the same," Gogun replied, handing her a bunch of leafy green shoots. "Some succor root for your journey home."

Claire hugged the old Troll, then rejoined Toby, Blinky, and AAARRRGGHH!!!

"So how does it feel to be the Trollhunter after all, Gogun?" asked Jim.

"Eh, it's . . . not terrible," Gogun conceded. "As a matter of fact, I've got an urge to perform some form of victory dance. Unless that sort of thing is now forbidden?"

"That's up to you," said Jim. "Your world's experienced enough heaviness lately. Maybe it's time for a role model who *isn't* like other Trolls. One with more of a . . . gentle touch."

"Hmm, Gogun the Gentle," said the old Troll, trying out the title. "I like it."

"Goodbye, Gogun the Gentle," Jim called as he took his place next to his friends.

"Farewell, Trollhunter of tomorrow," replied Gogun, his hand over his Amulet in salute.

Claire pointed her staff at the glitching Kairosect, then yelled, "Clonk-donk!"

A black hole opened and mingled with the buzzing temporal energies. One by one, it swept up Toby, Blinky, AAARRRGGHH!!!, Claire, and, finally, Jim. As the portal closed around him, Jim waved one last time. Gogun held up Shmorkrarg and wiggled her paw with his hand, making it look like the kitten was waving back.

"Later, Shmorkie," said Jim before his body left the Dark Ages and crossed into the infinite uncertainty of the Shadow Realm.

ONE FOR THE HISTORY BOOKS . . .

Microwaved burritos never tasted this good to Jim.

He and the rest of Team Trollhunters had made it back to the present famished and exhausted. After all, they'd been stuck in the Dark Ages for days—even though it seemed to the rest of the world that they were only gone for hours.

The Trolls in the warehouse, having just returned there via Strickler's secret path, rejoiced at the sight of their Trollhunter and his friends. They hailed Blinky as their leader and cheered even louder when Claire's portal sucked up Kilfred and his four followers.

As they were shooed back to the past, Kilfred—who had been left rather traumatized by his visit to Arcadia—decided two things: One, he was cutting humans from his diet and going full-on vegetarian forthwith. And two, he was retiring from advising Trolls on how to live their lives.

Once again the cosmic balance had been restored, and the warehouse Trolls handed out mugs of glug to toast this fact—even if they didn't fully understand the space-time mechanics behind it. The members of Team Trollhunters, however, weren't feeling up to a party at the moment.

Blinky remembered how his older brother, Dictatious, had been so kind during their child-hood, only to turn so sinister later in life. The six-eyed Troll wondered if he'd ever be able to forgive his misguided sibling, given the chance.

AAARRRGGHH!!! found himself similarly lost in thought, despite the rowdy Troll celebration around him. He knew his younger self would eventually break from the Gumm-Gumms at the Battle of Killahead Bridge and join the side of good. Yet AAARRRGGHH!!! now wondered if he was truly free of their tainted influence or if he would one day be counted among the Gumm-Gumms' ranks again. The gentle giant assumed only time would tell.

Toby also bowed out of the Troll festivities uncharacteristically early so he could hightail it to his orthodontist. He figured Dr. Muelas would need to replace the dental wire *ahora* if Toby wanted to have his braces off sometime this century.

Claire left the warehouse not too long after Toby to make a doctor's appointment of her own. She decided to take Jim's advice and schedule a physical with Dr. Lake. Claire's cough had worsened, and Gogun's succor root wasn't of much help now. The plant had mysteriously withered and died as she and her teammates traveled through the Shadow Realm on their way home. Claire could have sworn she saw a woman's hand reach out of the darkness and graze the medicinal herbs with her fingernail. But that was probably just Claire's fever playing tricks on her brain. . . .

Which left Jim. He excused himself from the warehouse with a yawn and rode his Vespa down sunlit Main Street, stopping only once to ogle at the blackened skeleton of Alex's Arcade. Parking in his garage, Jim ran into the kitchen ready to whip up that polenta, mushroom, and kale feast he'd been itching to cook for ages—literally. But as soon as he tied on his apron, a wave of exhaustion hit Jim harder than Orlagk's head-butt.

Fortunately, his mom also came home a minute later, after having been called back to the hospital for an emergency night shift. Barbara nuked two burritos in the microwave, and she and Jim ate them right there on the kitchen island. Mother and son were too tired to talk. They merely chewed in silence, enjoying the presence of each other's company nonetheless.

It was probably the greatest dinner/breakfast Jim Lake Jr. ever ate.

Eli's empty stomach grumbled, which only sounded louder in his current location inside of a high school locker. Steve yelled from the next locker over, pounding his fist on the metal wall between them. The racket caught the attention of Detective Scott, who opened both lockers and stepped aside as the Creepslayerz fell out.

The police had arrived at Arcadia Oaks High School after receiving several noise complaints—and after putting out the last of the fires on Main Street. Detective Scott and his fellow officers listened to Steve Palchuk's convincing testimony about the previous night. Between theatrical sobs,

Steve said that he and Eli had been studying late at night in the school library when a roving gang of punks from Arcadia Oaks Academy broke in.

Taking over the next part of their rehearsed alibi, Eli claimed that the Academy kids—still angry about losing the regional soccer championship—shoved him and Steve into the lockers, then vandalized the high school. After Detective Scott thanked the boys for their help and sent them home, the Creepslayerz privately shared another one of their special handshakes.

In the days that it took the city to repair their school, Steve and Eli kept tabs on the three Changelings they had encountered. They documented Strickler now taking meetings with Jim whenever Dr. Barbara Lake was away.

The Creepslayerz also spied NotEnrique taking dozens of "Vote Nuñez" lawn signs from his adoptive family's home to the Troll warehouse. The little green imp and Blinky cast warding spells over each sign and staked them across town to keep the Gumm-Gumms from ever finding the Troll hideout. Apparently, NotEnrique had gotten the idea after reading Eli's *Monsters & Mazes* playbook.

Steve and Eli also paid regular visits to the history museum. They told each other it was because they didn't trust Ms. Nomura—who had resumed her old job as a docent in the European antiquities wing after a long sabbatical—although it might have had more to do with the fact that the Creepslayerz were also teenaged boys. Of course, Steve and Eli would have no way of knowing this part but, one day, Nomura noticed something in the museum that she hadn't before. The Changeling had been restoring a tapestry, which depicted an epic battle from the Dark Ages, when she saw an odd detail stitched into the fabric. It was the small figure of a knight battling two gruesome monsters, his armor as white as a star.

Orlagk the Oppressor cursed the white knight as he staggered back to his army's camp, but the words came out as gibberish through his busted jaw. The besieged Gumm-Gumm king had expected a hero's welcome from his soldiers. Instead, he found only Gunmar and Bular, dark ambition apparent in their leering stares.

In his weakened condition, Orlagk was no

match for the traitorous father and son. He only managed to remove one of Gunmar's eyes before the howling-mad usurper removed Orlagk's head.

Bular kneeled before his father, and the new ruler of the Gumm-Gumms summoned the Decimaar Blade into his own twisted claw. Although Gunmar the Black's remaining eye did not see it at the time, his sword's pale glow fell upon a hidden witness to the betrayal.

From the shadows, a Gumm-Gumm named Skarlagk vowed to avenge her slain father, her young heart now hardened with scorn.

Gogun and Tellad-Urr saw this defining moment and many more from the Void. All Merlin's champions appeared in this strange afterlife following their final battles, although Gogun was the only Trollhunter to pass in his sleep—gently—from extreme old age. Since his arrival into this murky realm, Gogun had become friends with Tellad-Urr, the pair bonding over shared experiences with their human successor, Jim.

Gogun and Tellad-Urr's souls turned to another of the Void's scrying windows, which granted them a glimpse of the current Trollhunter training in his basement under Strickler's watchful yellow eyes.

"This bodes ill for the human child," Tellad-Urr the Terrible said, watching Jim take pointers from his Changeling tutor. "I know all too well the temptations of the dark path. This Impure may lead him onto it with his lies."

"I wouldn't be so sure of that," argued Gogun the Gentle. "Kim has a stout heart. It gave him strength even when the Amulet wouldn't. His very humanity shall serve as the compass to guide him through the deadliest trial he'll ever endure."

The two ghostly Trollhunters then faced a third scrying window. This one revealed a total solar eclipse, with the entire surface world in flames beneath the blackened firmament.

"The Eternal Night," spoke Tellad-Urr. "The end of all things."

"Perhaps," said Gogun's spirit, smiling at the thought of the human Trollhunter who had already brought light to another dark age. "Or perhaps it's the start of a new adventure. . . ."